Fading Hope

Copyright 2014

Rebecca Besser

Eli Constant

Morgan Garcia

Thea Gregory

Claire C. Riley

Armand Rosamilia

Jack Wallen

This book is a work of fiction. Unless otherwise noted, names, characters, places, and incidents are products of the author's imagination or are used fictitiously (unless otherwise noted). Any resemblance to actual locales, events or persons living or dead is entirely coincidental.

All rights reserved. No part of this book may be reproduced, scanned, or distributed in any printed or electronic format without express permission from the author. Please do not participate or encourage piracy of copyrighted materials in violation of the author's rights. Purchase only authorized editions.

Rebecca Besser

Introduction to "When Plans Fail" by Rebecca Besser

When I sat down to write this story, I thought about what hope was and what would make hope turn into hopelessness. For most people, our biggest hope is the future. And the biggest symbol of the future is a young child. I think every human being on the planet can look at any child and feel some kind of hope. We have hopes that the next generation will grow big and strong and handle things better than we did, if nothing else.

That hope is doubled, if not tripled, for a parent. They have love backing their hope that their child will have the chance to grow and experience life to the fullest. The hope starts when the parents find out the child has been conceived and it doesn't end until the moment the child's life ends (something every parent prays they don't have to face).

I wanted to harness that innocent and universal sense of hope in my story. I wanted to show the true end of humanity through the purest sense of hope when it all comes crashing down. After all, the human race can't continue without another generation, correct?

In "When Plans Fail" I give you a mother – one who has hope for her life and that of her son's. I insert them into the zombie apocalypse a few months after hell broke loose and society crumbled. There's nothing left around them, just an abandoned neighborhood.

Even though everything that was once normal is now dissolved to nothing, she clings to the hope that she can keep both of them alive by her sheer determination and her plans.

Simple things, like supplies, become an incredible complication when she has to figure out how to collect them when she is all alone with a small child. Who will babysit while she faces zombies to get food? Should she take the child with her and risk his noise and possible tears? Or should she leave him behind to fend for himself and hope no one or nothing finds him?

What would you choose?

It doesn't really matter...because the situation is completely hopeless. It's one of those "damned if you do/damned if you don't" situations that are very much a part of real life.

As you read "When Plans Fail," I hope you can put yourself in the mother's shoes and imagine the complex decisions she has to make, even though they seem so simple. I hope that deep down, you understand what drives her and makes her do what she does. I hope that when all her plans fail and she has to make the hardest choice of all, you understand the hopelessness that was there from the beginning.

When Plans Fail

The pantry is almost empty, Rachel thought for the hundredth time in the last hour. The sleeping infant in her arms was a heavy weight on her consciousness. She knew she had to do something if she and her small son were to survive.

She'd been lucky so far...she hadn't had to make a supply run in the six months since the world had fallen apart. She was happy now that her husband believed in being prepared for anything – that's what the military had done for him. The fact that he'd been on the other side of the world at the worst time ever was unfortunate; she could have used someone to help her, especially right now. She didn't want to take Troy out into the world. They'd barely made it back to the house when everything had gone wrong. She hadn't seen the zombies that the news and everyone else were talking about. All she'd seen was the chaos the idea of them had caused to society.

Everyone had been panicked and started looting, not caring about the people around them. She'd watched, helpless, as Mrs. Helton – the ninety-year-old woman who lived at the end of her street – was mowed down by a pickup truck in the super market parking lot.

The frail woman had been thrown by the strike and had flown through the air to land on the hood of a vehicle traveling the other direction; she hadn't stood a chance and Rachel had hoped that she'd died instantly. She'd been too afraid to get out and check on the woman, for fear of something happening to herself or Troy (who'd been only one month old).

Just the thought of losing Troy made her clutch him harder, closer to her chest, which caused him to stir.

"Shhhh," she whispered instantly, trying to keep him quiet. She was always trying to keep him quiet.

How am I going to keep him quiet out in the open? she wondered silently and almost started to cry as panic choked her.

She vowed then and there not to take him out unless she had to – she would wait until she absolutely had to leave the safety of the basement beneath their house before she did, before she would risk either of their lives.

*

Four days later...

Rachel stared at the bare shelves in the pantry, knowing she now had to leave their sanctuary and face the world in whatever state it may be. She wasn't looking forward to it. Troy *had* been cranky for the last couple days, fussing and crying more than normal. For once in her life, she wished she had something, like a drug, to make him sleep and keep him quiet.

She'd always hated the idea of doing something like that to one's child, but she felt that she had good reason to do so, only she didn't have the necessities.

She'd made a solid plan, or so she thought, of how she could go out and get supplies with the least amount of risk. She'd kept Troy awake for a long time – over fifteen hours if she'd calculated correctly – now she was waiting for him to fall asleep.

Her plan was to leave him in the safety of the basement while she went out into the neighborhood and raided the closest houses, especially the ones she knew small children had lived in. Deep down, she felt bad about hoping those families had left...or died. But she reasoned that she and her son needed to survive and that was her main concern. The only thing she wasn't sure about was whether she could kill another living human being to ensure the survival of herself and her son.

She could hear Troy fussing in his crib, and she moved toward him.

He sat up and raised his arms toward her.

She smiled and picked him up. Humming softly, she walked around the limited area, holding him close; it didn't take him long to fall asleep.

Rachel kissed Troy on his sweet, soft head with tears running down her cheeks.

"I love you," she whispered, and laid him back into his crib. For a moment she just stared down at him, silently vowing to return to him no matter what it took. Finally, through a force of will and despite her paralyzing fear of never seeing him again, she made her muscles move and she walked to the door.

The simple barricade bar wasn't hard to remove, but it still took her time. She was trying to be extra quiet so she wouldn't wake Troy. Once she managed it, she twisted the doorknob and started to open the door – it creaked loudly.

Rachel froze and listened for any noise behind her from Troy and for any sounds from beyond the door. When there was neither, she continued to open the door as slowly and quietly as she could. Once she had it all the way open, she held her breath and listened again.

Tears were no longer flowing silently down her face, but she was still terrified of what she was doing by leaving her baby to fend for himself, and of where she was going...into God knew what.

She could hear nothing more than Troy's even breaths as he slept. She stepped through the doorway and onto the stairs that would take her up to the ground floor of the house, pulling the door closed behind her.

She carried the metal barricade bar up the stairs with her, and gasped when she almost dropped it at the top; it thudded loudly against the wood timbers of the wall of the stairwell, but she managed to keep hold of it.

This too cost her time, since she felt she had to wait to see if anything beyond the doorway leading into the house had heard her.

Nothing...again.

She said a silent prayer that her luck would continue, and that she would face nothing but quiet emptiness the entire supply run. She knew it was unlikely to be true, but she couldn't help but hope.

Rachel followed the same precautionary routine that she had with the lower door as she opened the upper door that led directly into the kitchen on the ground floor of the house. Everything was still silent, so she closed the upper door behind.

She looked at the bar she'd hefted up the stairs and the door she'd just closed. Her plan had been to somehow secure this door with it to keep Troy safe, but she saw no way to do so affectively. At last, in desperation, she maneuvered a heavy wooden table from the corner in front of the door to at least make it difficult for any zombies to get to Troy.

She knew that a human would be smart enough to know that the table was blocking the doorway – she just hoped if someone did happen through and see it, they wouldn't feel the urge to explore further. She stood the metal bar under the table, behind a leg. No one would see it there.

Her hopes were no more than threads of chance. She knew this, but still she clung to those threads for dear life.

She moved through the house as soundlessly as possible, heading upstairs to retrieve a duffel bag from the master bedroom closet. While there, she decided to look out the upstairs window, seeking the vantage point to give her an idea of what she faced outside.

The blinds had been drawn by her previously to prevent anyone, or anything, from seeing movement within. Light seeped around the edges and through the cracks just enough to let her see the gray shapes of the furniture around her. When she slipped a finger around the edge and pulled ever so slightly and slowly, she was blinded by a flash of sunlight. She winced and blinked rapidly until her eyes adjusted.

What she saw beyond was not what she'd expected. Weeds had choked all the once well-manicured lawns beyond recognition. The once desired and family-friendly neighborhood now looked worse than the slums she'd seen over her twenty-seven years. She didn't know what she'd expect to see, but this shocked her. Facing reality, she knew no one would be mowing or working on the upkeep of their houses, but she hadn't expected it to look so bad, so swiftly.

Cars were abandoned on the street and in various yards. The weeds and vegetation that had grown up and around the ones in the yards shadowed the insides of the vehicles. Any treasures within the metal hulks were hidden from sight.

She knew there might be something of value or interest in them, especially the trunks, but she would save those until dusk, when there was less chance of her movements in the open to be seen.

In every direction she could see, as far as she could see, there was no movement save the wind as it breezed through, ruffling the foliage that had overgrown the world in its eagerness to erase mankind. This brought a measure of calm over Rachel, and she almost decided not to bring what else she'd retrieved from the closet...a 9mm Glock.

Henry, her husband, had made sure she'd known how to use the pistol, telling her that with him away she might need it for her protection. Her aptitude with the weapon came as a fortunate surprise.

With another deep breath that she exhaled on a sigh, she resigned herself to get on with her task so she could return to Troy before he awoke and found her missing.

Faster than she'd come upstairs, she was again downstairs and stood before the front door. She reached her hand out to open it when she suddenly thought better, and headed to the back door. If there was anything outside, she wanted to be the one with the advantage of surprise.

The back door was the better choice, but was stiff and hard to open from the months of neglect. She made it outside and stood for a moment just breathing in the forgotten scent of fresh air; it seemed like a lifetime since her lungs had filled with a sun-kissed breath. She could smell the wild flowers that were weeds as she inhaled deeply a few times. Despite herself, she smiled. Being outside was a blessing she hadn't counted in all her dread.

With a grin on her face, she tromped across the small porch, down the steps, and into the overgrown yard. She planned to visit three doors down where a family with triplets had lived. At the time, she'd thought that caring for so many babies at once was crazy, now she hoped they had enough stock of formula and other baby foods to keep Troy content until he started eating adult foods. Even then, she knew those would be hard to come by. She'd already given him some that she thought he could handle, mashing canned food to make it easier for him to consume. He choked sometimes and she felt bad, but she didn't know what else to do. She planned to remedy their troubles and she prayed as she slunk from house to house that she would meet with success.

When Rachel reached the house she desired, the broken widows and wide open door made her hope sink like a stone to the pit of her stomach. Still, she walked up the stairs that led to the back door of the home and entered. Her footfalls were silent, her breath coming in small tight gasps.

She didn't know what to expect, and she'd only been in the house once before for the baby shower. She was pleased to see that the door entered into the kitchen, similar to her own home. She instantly went to the cabinets and opened them.

They were empty.

With a sigh, she moved to the pantry, still nothing. All the shelves were completely bare. There were two more places she knew she would have to check before she left: the nursery and the basement. If anything was still here to be found, it would be in one of those places, she was sure.

Rachel stood still in the kitchen and listened for any noise from within the house. There was a small creak and a distant, dull, rhythmic bang, but nothing seemed immediate or particularly dangerous.

She headed upstairs to where she knew the nursery would be, on the second floor. The banging sound increased in its intensity, but she wasn't overly concerned.

When she made it to the top of the stairs, she saw what was making the noise – a door stood ajar and was banging on the wall from a slight breeze coming through an open window she spied just beyond when the door moved.

The room the door belonged to appeared to be the master bedroom, so she chose the door closest to it, turned the knob, pushed the door open, and entered the room.

Her hand instantly rose to her mouth as a gasp escaped her lips. She'd found the nursery...and wished she hadn't.

Everything was coated with dark dried blood, and little bones lay everywhere with thin, dried scraps of meat still clinging to them. There were enough of them to be all three of the babies who had once slept in the room.

Rachel gagged and tried to blink away the tears that sprang to her eyes. She backed toward the door with her eyes darting about in panic and horror; they fell on a shelf in the far corner with five large cans of powdered baby formula. She paused. She needed it. Troy needed it.

She schooled her emotions the very best she could and willed herself to step over the haunts of carnage and move toward what she'd come for. With shaking hands, she lifted and inserted the cans into the empty bag she carried.

There was a slight creak behind her, which she assumed was the door in the breeze from the hallway, so she paid it no mind. Once she turned, she realized the mistake she'd made in her complacency and grief.

In the doorway, swaying slightly from side to side were the forms of the slain triplets' parents. Rachel only knew it was them by the ripped and stained clothing that hung from their forms; it was familiar. They faces were decayed to the point of being unrecognizable.

"Oh, God," Rachel breathed, struggling around the bag's shoulder strap to reach the pistol she had strapped to her side.

Upon her utterance, they growled and darted toward her with their arms outstretched.

Rachel dropped the bag of formula, raised the pistol, and discharged a round into the head of the male zombie.

Stepping back quickly to take aim at the other zombie, she tripped over the straps of the duffel bag and fell into the rotted remains of one of the babies. She flinched, knowing what lay beneath her.

In that moment, as her eyes blinked, the zombie-woman dove down over her.

Rachel swung the gun up to defend herself and the zombie grabbed her arm and bit her wrist.

She screamed as pain vibrated through her arm, and kicked the undead mother away. She whipped the pistol up and fired two quick shots that hit the zombie woman in the neck and head. She went down hard.

Blood was flowing freely from Rachel's arm; the wound was deep. She looked around for something, anything to staunch the flow.

Her mind refused to accept what had just happened and offered up a single directive – patching herself up enough to make it back to Troy. She blocked out what the bite meant, hoping against the inevitable that things would be okay. She'd seen zombie movies. She knew to shoot them in the head, and she knew bites transferred the infection to new specimens. She'd also heard those same things in the news, verifying the myths of horror.

She found a baby blanket under her leg, tore it into strips, and then wrapped it around her wrist.

Rachel was light-headed from blood loss and pain. Once her wound was wrapped, she allowed herself to fall back and lay down. Tears ran freely from her eyes. Her imagination told her what dark things had transpired in this house, this very room, months before... The parents had become zombies, the father probably bringing the sickness home when he returned from work, attacking his wife once he'd succumb. Together, they'd eaten their young. The very idea made her sick to her stomach, but she knew that if she returned to Troy, having been bitten herself, she would do the same thing.

As she lay there, she came up with a plan. The plan had less threads of hope than the one she'd set out to preform today; it would be more precarious and she would have to hurry if it were to have a chance at success.

*

Rachel stumbled back downstairs with the duffel bag half full of cans of powdered formula. Zombies were everywhere on the ground level, having been drawn by the sound of gunfire. None of them showed her any attention past a quick sniff; they recognized her as one of their own. She was glad of this, but saddened by it at the same time.

Their indifference made it easier for her to make her way home, but made it clear that she was quickly being taken over by the zombie infection.

She would soon be one of them... too soon.

She couldn't believe how many of them there were, when before, she'd seen none. By her estimation there were close to a hundred zombies now roaming the street between her house and the one where she'd been. The danger that had lurked around her had been more real than she'd understood. Her feeble attempt at finding supplies had been doomed from the beginning.

She made her way back to her house as fast as she possibly could. When she arrived, she found everything as she had left it. She was weak from blood loss and fever and it took her longer to move the table out of the way than it had previously, but she still managed; she completely ignored the barricade bar that clattered loudly on the floor. Her plan ran in a jumbled sequence through her mind, and she applied all of her focus to preforming it.

She took none of the care now that she'd shown before. She practically ran down the stairs to the basement and burst through the door to see that Troy was still sleeping.

Quickly, she scooped him and his blanket up and charged back up the stairs, stumbling slightly near the top; she reached out and steadied herself against the wall for a moment to regain her balance.

Troy stirred in her arms, but didn't fully awaken. Her touch and her scent were familiar to him, so he wasn't alarmed at being moved.

Rachel was grateful Troy stayed quiet; it was going to be hard enough to get him through the continuously growing crowd of the undead as it was. If he cried, it would be harder still.

Once she was again outside, she kept her distance and skirted as many of the zombies as she could. When she was away from most of them, she checked the cars in the street, one at a time, for keys hanging from the ignition. When she found one that looked promising, she gingerly opened the door, sat down in the driver's seat, and turned the key.

Nothing happened.

She choked down a sigh and moved forward, still searching for keys. After three more vain attempts, she found one that would start. The noise of the engine starting woke Troy, who began to cry. The noise of both turned most of the zombies, now a quarter mile away, in their direction. She didn't care though, since she and Troy began to move swiftly away in the car.

*

Rachel's vision was getting cloudy and she knew it wouldn't be long. But, much to her despair, she had found nothing to indicate the existence of other people who had survived. Her plan had been to turn Troy over to someone who could take care of him since she would no longer be able to.

She drove until she couldn't any longer. She felt herself growing weaker and the world further and further away.

She brought the car to a stop and stared out of the windshield. Troy had just woken up and was fussing. He grabbed at her and clutched her clothes in his small hands, snuggling close to her.

She could smell his blood...his life, and she wanted it. Her lips peeled back from her teeth and she hissed low and deep; it didn't faze Troy.

With a sob, she realized she was becoming as horrible as the couple who'd killed and eaten their own triplets. She didn't want to be like that. She didn't want her end, or Troy's, to be like that. She had failed to find a safe place for him, and now she was turning into one of the monsters she most feared. She didn't want Troy's end to be that violent... that painful.

Her options were limited. She knew she could keep him alive, despite her upcoming death and reanimation, but that would probably still lead to his death in the end. He would starve if she locked him inside the car with the hope that someone would find him before it was too late.

There was only one option left to them both; it would be the end to every dream and hope she'd ever had, but it was all her fevered brain could come up with.

Rachel pulled Troy into her arms, and rubbed her nose against his; he quieted at the gesture of comfort and love.

"I love you, sweetness," Rachel whispered as her other hand reached for the pistol at her side.

Before he could squirm, and before she could change her mind, she raised the gun, pressed the barrel to the back of Troy's head, and pulled the trigger.

The explosive sound of the gun firing a round was deafening in the confined space of the car.

Pain erupted from Rachel's ears and face, but the world didn't go dark as she'd expected.

The bullet didn't quite do as she'd wanted... The round had silenced her child forever, but had merely blown a hole in her cheek. She'd wanted a final end for them both.

In pain, in grief, with her ears ringing, she laid Troy's body on the seat beside her, averting her eyes from his face. With violently shaking hands, she slipped the barrel of the pistol in her mouth and closed her eyes. The metal vibrating against her teeth from her shaking hand resounded through her skull, until, on an exhale, she pulled the trigger, effectively ending her own life and ensuring she wouldn't eat the remains of her baby.

About Rebecca Besser

Rebecca Besser resides in Ohio with her wonderful husband and amazing son. They've come to accept her quirks as normal while she writes anything and everything that makes her inner demons squeal with delight. She's best known for her work in adult horror, but has been published in fiction, non-fiction, and poetry for a variety of age groups and genres. She's entirely too cute to be scary in person, so she turns to the page to instil fear into the hearts of the masses. She's currently seeking an agent with her first novel, Nurse Blood, with hopes to expand her reach of dread through a mass market publication in the future. Meanwhile, you can join her dark minions by learning more about her on her blog, Facebook page, or Twitter.

Eli Constant

Introduction to "Chick'n Soup for the Soul" By Eli Constant

When I signed on to write for Jack Wallen's project "Fading Hope", I was optimistic. I thought- "this is a fantastic premise/theme; I can come up with something stellar for this". Maybe optimism was the wrong way to approach this anthology, because I hit a roadblock. Right from the outset, I face-slammed into an impervious wall decorated with a singular, flashing sign that told me to quit and go back.

Each outline I jotted down, each story I began, felt forced and pedantic. I ended up crumpling a dozen virtual papers and tossing them into the great scrap-heap of the uninspired.

It took me a long time, and a story about crab men in a world gone ocean, to realize the problem. It took an epiphany.

I like optimism.

I like hope.

And I'm emotionally, morally, metaphysically adverse to the idea that hope can fade and flicker out.

So how does one go about writing a story that grates against the grain of belief? How does one abandon hope, when hope is so well-loved?

Simple.

I wrote a story that I hate.

I hated writing it. I hated the editing process.

And I hate reading it most of all.

Because even in the darkest of my stories, there's always some grain, some little light that whispers "hope". Even though the world is shit, hold on to hope. It's the only thing that keeps us from sinking into the gray of life and forgetting color.

So, enjoy this story that I truly, ardently, emphatically hate. And don't be surprised if you find, in the end, that I couldn't help but sneak in a small morsel of optimism.

Chick'n Soup for the Soul

Four other too-large bodies were squashed onto the bunk beside me.

The elevated bed was hardly big enough for two people, let alone five. No one ever complained though. Opening your mouth, uttering anything other than clipped words of subjugation... even the youngest among us knew that would be a mistake. And there were small children here, some barely five or six, trapped in these caged rooms, the doors of which all simultaneously opened only twice per day– allowing the occupants to stretch, to fight to use the 12-toilet facility, to try and find the loved ones scattered about the prison for a swift "hello" and embrace.

I'd long given up finding my cousin and aunt.

Each day, prisoners were taken by our captors. At first, I had thought them the lucky ones- freed from the cramped quarters and unsanitary conditions. They never came back, never had to live like this again. But then my mind had started imagining what horrors those "freed" folks must face.

So maybe I was lucky. Maybe.

Lucky to have two male and two female adult bodies pushing me into the concrete wall.

I used to love being petite. Now, I would give nearly anything to be a gigantic male bodybuilder– be like that guy four cells down who looked so large and mean that no one would go near him, so he got a big ol' bed all to himself.

I sat up and it took some force to extricate my body from the pile of adults pressed against me. Time was a non-existent here – at least in the 24-hour-cycle sense – but I knew it must be the food hour. I heard the distant clink of metal ladle against metal bowl. The slop they gave us wasn't much better than dog chow. My sense of taste was dead now, after a hundred and five meals of the exact same soupy, khaki-colored mess; I probably couldn't discern roachie fast food from prime steak at a Michelin Guide high-ranked restaurant. Steak. Beautifully pink, medium rare, cut-it-with-a-butter-knife steak. Okay... maybe my taste buds weren't totally dead.

Others were stirring now, moving hastily to kneel on the ground, hands outstretched for a bowl. They didn't give us utensils anymore– not since they realized even a spoon could be fashioned into a weapon of sorts.

We didn't really need forks or knives now, since our creepy-ass wardens further watered down the sludge. It was an easy thing to lift the bowl to the mouth, dribble in the mess, and then feel it slosh its sloppy way down toward the stomach.

You had to do it quickly or the flavor would hit your taste buds and it wouldn't stay long in your body. I'd learned that the hard way, wasting more than one serving of food to a discerning palate and overwhelming nausea.

I was the first in my cell to crouch on the floor and reach my fingers beneath the metal gate in a bid for a bowl. My "early bird gets the worm" attitude was rewarded with a swift kick to the gut. I gasped, bile building in my throat.

But I held my ground.

If I moved, I'd never get a bowl of food. Out of my periphery, I saw the foot rear back again, preparing to strike. Moving at the last moment, I bent my arm and targeted my assailant's knee with my too-thin, sharp elbow. I used all the force I could muster, which was pitiful, but it did the trick.

It was a matter of hitting at the right angle, knocking into the knee cap and forcing it to invert violently.

The sickening crack of bone was an interesting counterpoint to the metal-on-metal sound of a bowl being filled with food. Crack. Slop. Slosh.

The bowl was pushed under the gate and toward me. Metal against rock now, an ear-bleeding screech of sound.

A wail called my attention from the slop I was already drinking greedily. My attacker had been one of the adult males who shared my bunk, the one with stringy mouse-brown hair and touches of grey in his beard.

He was in the fetal position now, sobbing like a wounded bitch, nursing his broken- or at least fractured- knee joint. I didn't feel any sympathy for him; another thing our jailers had robbed me of was my sense of humanity. You couldn't be weak though, not here.

People had to see that you were tough, willing to draw blood to keep yourself alive. I'd tried another tactic all this time; I had acted docile and submissive. I was too tired for that shit now.

See? The lucky one. Learning to be strong; learning to fight.

I scrambled back quickly, dropping my already empty food bowl as the gate to our cell groaned open. My cell mates followed suit, until the lot of us were pressed against the walls of our cage. Two hulking figures entered, dressed, as always, in the head-to-toe hooded brown capes.

The material swirled about their bodies, creating the illusion that the figures changed shape, widened and then thinned, lengthened and then shortened. It was always disconcerting.

The man I'd injured screamed as one of the figures bent down and lifted him effortlessly. I saw no hands, just dark extensions of the cape.

The second figure did not move, although it seemed as if he were looking at all of us in the cell, one by one, reminding us that misbehavior or injury or *so many other things* could sentence us to whatever fate lay beyond the prison walls.

My body relaxed minutely as the entrance re-closed, protesting loudly. My remaining prison companions moved away from the walls; some bee-lined for the floor, where many had accidently spilled their soup in their haste to move away from the caped figures. Others, the more timid of our prison pack, crawled back onto their respective bunks.

The surrounding cells were eerily silent, save for the wet licking sounds emanating from those scavengers tonguing the soup-flavored floor. I stared at them for a moment. They were starved animals, their bodies pushing against one another as they humiliated themselves.

Did humiliation exist here? For me, it did. Hurting that man had reawakened other parts of me... like pride.

Disgusted, I returned to my own bed, taking my place against the hard wall. I knew the injured man would never return. It was a sick satisfaction to realize that I would have a little more sleeping room from now on.

I'd never had to be violent before. I was filled again with sick satisfaction, thinking about the girl hanging her head, keeping low, trying to stay invisible and survive.

I'd always been able to make ends meet, get a bowl of food or at least lick an empty bowl clean of sparse remnants.

In the time I'd been here – all those many meal hours of dog chow – I'd witnessed others protect themselves and assert their dominance. Those 'troublemakers' never lasted in the prison very long after that though. Guess I'd dug my own grave today. But it had felt good. *So damn good.* To stop being weak; it was like a balm for the soul, better than any homemade chicken soup. Today, I'd stopped being the youngest in my cell, the little sixteen year-old who could be bullied.

That feeling was worth a long walk off a short pier any day of the week. If I knew what day it was, I'd mark it on the calendar; maybe even draw a little stick figure of an injured man next to an overly-happy smiley face.

My parents wouldn't exactly be proud though- ever the pacifists, ever the protestors. They always believed that peace would find a way, that we'd learn how to coexist. But peace hadn't prevailed. It never would. And my parents' protestations were meaningless strings of nonsensical words in the din of world death.

In the end, my mom and dad had been a short piece on the six o'clock news. Small blips in an endless string of casualties. Everyone had known it was only a matter of time before someone got the upper hand, won the war and became the dominant power. The brutality which followed the end of the war made the years of fighting seem comparably tame.

Hours ticked by. Silently I counted- 1 Mississippi, 2 Mississippi, 3 Mississippi, until I reached 3,600 Mississippi. Then my brain would reset and I'd begin a new hour. Hushed voices filled the air. A scuffle sounded in the distance.

Finally, the cell doors swung open simultaneously, filling the building with deep grating bellows. I stayed motionless as people flooded out from their cells and into the prison corridor, pushing and shoving toward the bathroom facilities. Many didn't bother- their bed coverings long-soaked with urine and feces piled in a cell corner. I was happy my cellmates had not yet resorted to using our small space as a toilet. Well, except that one time- when the woman named Mary hadn't been able to hold her pee until the second bathroom visit.

She'd been so embarrassed, standing against the gate, willing it to swing open so she could race to the facilities and wash herself in the dingy water from one of the stained toilet bowls. There weren't any sinks or mirrors, just a line of twelve nasty toilets, no walls, and no doors to provide modesty.

Mary had lasted only five meals; the cloaked figures had taken her away and she'd almost seemed relieved. There never seemed to be any rhyme or reason to who our captors took. There were a few obvious instances of course- they weeded out the injured ones and the violent ones. Meaning- the man I'd taught a lesson to and me being the lesson-giving rabble-rouser.

They'd come for me soon. Empty bladder and rumbling stomach. I was on the hit list.

An angry, bestial scream shot through the dim prison building. Then shouting, mangled words spoken by hoarse voices.

"I was next in line, bitch."

"Get out of my way, old man."

"I'll give you old man."

"Stop it. Stop. You're going to get all of us in trouble."

"Please, I just want to pee and get back to my cell."

I didn't really see how anyone could need to use the restroom. The soupy food provided just enough water and nutrition to keep us alive. There shouldn't be any excess. I usually tried to muscle my way to a toilet, sit down and push, just in case, but I didn't see the point today. I just didn't see the point. Not with the shouting and screaming.

The dim lights above our head flashed twice and then everything went dark. That lasted ten Mississippi counts and then the red strobe began to pulse, warning everyone to return to their cells as quickly as possible.

"Son of a..."

"I freaking told you! I told you we'd get in trouble."

"I didn't get to pee."

That last voice sounded so sad, so resigned. It made a sharp pang shoot through my chest.

Scrambling. Shoving. Shouting. The prison filled with the rush and bustle of people trying to get back to their respective cells.

The pulsing crimson light gave me glimpses of faces shoved into metal bars and folks being knocked to the floor. They never gave us long to comply.

Fifteen Mississippi counts and the cell gates began to swing shut. The strobe died away and was once again replaced by the dim fluorescents.

Figures were pacing the hall between the cells now, forcibly dragging stragglers out of the prison. Some of the people fought, others let themselves be hauled away without a fight, as if they were ready for the end. Part of me didn't blame them. We'd lived like wild animals for too long. Maybe giving in, giving up, maybe that was the only way to find a shred of humanity and civility again.

Nah. I thought derisively. *Humanity has never been all peaches and cream. More often than not, humanity's a pinch of nice with a whole lot of bitchiness tossed into the mix.* That's what our captors would never understand.

We might seem defeated. We might have our moments of exhausted self-indulgence, but eventually, when the defeatism ran its course, we'd be back in the saddle and ready to wield a weapon.

My uncle used to say something to that effect – "when the saddle busts a strap, bareback is better than walking". Okay, maybe that wasn't exactly the same thing as defeating defeatism, but it was definitely about optimism.

I almost laughed out loud. I'd seen my uncle die. There'd been nothing optimistic about it. Head severed from shoulders, fingers flexing mechanically as the last directions from the brain ran their course. That was the image I closed my eyes to. It flitted behind my eyelids, flashes of death and running.

I'd been staying with my aunt, uncle, and cousin the weekend everything went to shit. Mom and Dad were up to their usual antics- picketing a factory in Bealeton that underpaid and overworked its staff. I was ten; my cousin Noah was eight and a royal pain in the butt.

He and I were fighting over the television remote when we'd heard a crash. Not a normal car-against-car impact, but a sort of earthy thump against the ground and the sound that wood makes when it splits- sort of a crunch crossed with a crack. Then finally, a splash.

When we had all tumbled out of the French doors that led to the stone patio, we'd had to rub our eyes in disbelief. A gun metal gray pod bobbed up and down in the pool. A section of the white picket fence surrounding the chlorinated, pale blue water lay broken and mangled. Uncle John was backing toward us, screaming for us to get back in the house.

That's when the pod had opened; the hatch appeared like a swift beam of light cutting a round portal. That illuminated circle of pod wall slid up and over soundlessly across the dark metal. Two figures had appeared then, their features completely obscured, standing inside the pod, rising and falling as their craft moved in the water. Aunt April pushed me and Noah back into the house, keeping the door open for Uncle John.

But he hadn't made it.

One of the figures had raised an appendage which wielded a small object- almost like a miniature LED flashlight. It made no sound, emitted no visible beam or projectile, but just the same, my Uncle John- once so alive and quirky, full of funny sayings and sage advice- became headless.

His head rolled down his torso, landing with a plop against the stone; the impact was enough to make a Rorschach splatter against the light gray pavers.

His body twitched for a moment before collapsing sideways- his lower half splayed across the stone patio, his upper half across the grass.

Aunt April had been uncharacteristically level-headed, responding opposite her nature to seeing her headless husband writhing on the back yard lawn, crimson coloring the bright green grass he'd lovingly cared for year after year. I'd expected her to scream, sob, push away from us and toward Uncle John's body, but she hadn't. For my part, I'd been too shocked to show any emotional response. My cousin was another story. He'd just kept yelling "daddy" over and over. For once in his measly life, I'd felt sorry for him.

We probably should have died that day, but our attackers had taken some time to exit the pod and find footing on the pool decking. Then they had been unabashedly fascinated by Uncle John's inert body. They'd stood over him, running this flat, clear rectangle over his body that 'bipped' and 'booped'.

I'd wanted to see their faces... monsters are never as scary when you can see their faces and call them by name.

There hadn't been any time. And I wasn't stupid enough to run over to Uncle John's killers and ask them politely to remove their face covering.

We'd fled with just the gas in Aunt April's tiny hybrid car and the clothes on our backs. She had taken me straight back to my parents three hours away. We had stayed with them for a short time... long enough for them to never come back from a peace protest, long enough to see the news piece. Think 'maybe they come in peace'- hand shake, miscommunication, explosion. It was a B-rated horror flick made reality.

Aunt April kept me and my cousin alive and free for almost six years. A lifetime in terms of war and foraging.

One thing had always haunted me during those six years though. It still haunted me now.

No one had ever seen their faces, their hands, their feet. They were always covered, masked by the folds of that alien dark cloth that undulated with repressed life. Just a single photo, a blurred image of features, would have been enough to calm the nightmares.

As I bled back into wakefulness, dim light made me see a dark orange-red through my still-closed lids. My body felt strange; I hardly even felt the stone wall against me. I was always smashed into it, the other bodies piled against and on top. Only three bodies now, I reminded myself.

But the absence of one person could not make such room. Stretching my arm out and feeling the brittle, stained mattress beneath me, I finally opened my eyes and realized I was alone on the bed.

Alone. I was sleeping on the bunk alone. For the first time in one hundred and six meals, I'd slept soundly by my lonesome; there was no too-close-for-comfort foul body odor mixing with my own or multiple bodies sweating and emitting fear pheromones.

There was no calloused male hand reaching out while I slept, groping for the intimate parts of me. More than one girl had been raped here. Our captors didn't seem to care. I'd avoided it so far– by not fighting, by allowing the little touches and whispers, the noses sniffing deeply at the crook of my neck.

Yes, my heart had thumped wildly during these encounters; my hands had balled into livid fists. Yet I had endured and so had my teenage, middle-of-an-apocalypse, between-the-legs innocence. *Whoop-de-doo.* A lot of good it did me. Some of the men would trade their soupy, gross rations for a little "affection".

If I'd been slutty the past hundred and six meals, I might have ended every mealtime twice as full. If I'd been a bone-breaking bitch early on, I might have been long-accustomed to sleeping comfortably. Course... I might also have been long-dragged away and faced my fate. Like I said- troublemakers never lasted long after first violence. Guess I should restart my meal count and see how many days I make it.

A clinking in the distance alerted me to chowtime.

It was the nasty slop hour again.

Had it been a whole day already? That meant I'd missed second bathroom time. My mind turned to my bladder. Surely even with the small amount of moisture entering my body, I'd need to urinate by now? But no. I felt no pressure in my lower stomach, no need to clench and hold, waiting desperately for the cages to all swing open.

Like clenching and holding and praying you wouldn't wet yourself would do you any good fighting through the unrelenting hoards pushing toward the line of not-so-porcelain-white-anymore thrones.

Food was worth getting out of bed for. Maybe nasty toilets weren't, but food sure as hell was.

I wasn't the first to crouch on the floor this time, but once I did, the other occupants gave me wide berth. I almost smirked, the self-satisfied teenager finding a way to be cocky. An abnormal feeling. I liked it. Another sick satisfaction. Another result of viciousness.

My head tilted and I lifted the bowl to my mouth; I slurped happily, reveling in my new found status as the bad girl in my cell. The food was almost palatable today, like someone had accidently added more salt and a dash of decent cooking.

So unusually content was I, that the protesting groan of the opening cell gate did not alarm me. It should have. I was nearly half-smiling as I lowered the bowl from my face, automatically using the gross right sleeve of my too-big shirt to wipe away the remnants of slop from the corners of my mouth.

My face fell in disbelief as the two rippling, cloaked figures came toward me.

No... no... it was only yesterday! People have lasted nearly a week after being violent in here! Not now. I don't want to go now! Not when I've finally found my place here, finally stopped being the worthless, invisible bottom of the damn food chain.

Every bit of me wanted to kick and scream– do everything I could to keep them from taking me. But it seemed that my fighting skills were specialized for old men trying to deny me food. Big, brave, badass girl I was.

The figures carried me between them, my petite frame a feather pillow to the strength in their muscles. My toes barely skimmed the ground. I was a dead fish, my body limp noodle, already cooked and ready for marinara.

We passed through a set of doors and entered a room even less well-lit than the prison. A million and one thoughts traipsed through my mind, trying to find foothold in my phobias.

What the hell had I done? Risked everything for food, not even food really, just a watered down mess of crap. It was stupid of me. In the world of things to risk your neck for, I'd picked food. Not love or family or freedom. Food.

Our movements stopped in the center of that room. The light was so dim; I could only see shadows, illusions of things. A hysterical giggle escaped me. Illusions. It was all illusion. The figures and their damnable cloaks were illusion. Everything was fake. I wasn't going to die. Not like this.

I was smashed against the concrete wall, lying in the bunk, still sharing it with four other bodies, feeling a hand reach for my boob. Yep. *Dreaming this illusion that would end me.* I giggled again. A 16 year-old poet in a prison about to be killed by aliens. Awesome.

My eyelids fluttered as something pressed against my face. I involuntarily inhaled, sucking in a deep breath of slightly sweet-smelling, but somehow, rancid gas that instantly fogged the clear gas mask; a gloved hand held it in position firmly, keeping me from dislodging it and escaping the noxious odor.

I couldn't keep my eyes open. Collapsing awkwardly, I felt strong hands grip me beneath the armpits. Other hands took hold of my ankles. Before I slipped into sleep, I felt the length of my body laid against the softest mattress I'd felt in years.

If this was death, call a funeral home and pick me out a box. It was all a-ok with... me...

I woke up.

Why did I have to wake up?

I'd had the best dreams, the most exquisite, incandescent, beautiful dreams.

Green grass, the sun over my head, my grandparents, long dead, singing in the kitchen, their voices carrying out to where I lounged on the ground. Pop-pop's favorite tattered towel rolled under my head for a makeshift pillow.

A glass of Me-maw's homemade lemonade in a tall glass with so much ice that the sides of the glass were coated in a waterfall of condensation sat beside me- on the only level piece of grass near where I was.

I had on my favorite dress too, one that I'd outgrown, but refused to donate, despite my mother's urgings. I wore bicycle shorts with it. It was perfect. A perfect summer day when I was seven. I loved that farm, my grandparents, the way the cow pastures smelled in the heat of summer.

Why did I have to wake up?

It was the worst type of cruelty. After all I'd been through; this was the pinnacle, the final nail, the torture that made everything else seem so minor.

My eyes opened then and my mind was filled with a hyper-realistic sensation, a washing-through, like my brain was on rinse cycle and was never going to stop.

Water was churning from left side brain to right, a rushing river relentlessly hitting the inner walls of my skull, flushing out the little nuances of myself, stripping away the memories of past happiness, memories of survival, memories of the desperation in the prison.

I began to forget.

The way the pastures smelled in summer.

That odd way the gold flecks in my father's eyes had always caught the sun and sparkled like crazy.

How I longed for the taste of a well-cooked steak.

And the feel of the oh-so-soft bed beneath my body.

It was all seeping away, the little snapshots, the tendrils of feelings from a past life.

Lifting a hand to my face, I saw a glove. My body vibrated in terror, thinking it was the covered hand of one of the figures. But, no.

It responded to my commands, the fingers flexing, the hand waving in front of my eyes. It was my own hand, my petite digits coated in dark fabric. Sitting up, I looked around, realizing that I could see in the dimness well, my head covered by a breathable mask, night vision incorporated into the black lenses sewn into the face covering.

Around me, over a dozen people lay on other hospital cots. Some were cloaked like the figures... like me... others were stark naked, not even the smallest of modest coverings over their private parts. As I sat, a door that I had not noticed yet swung inward and admitted a figure, the alien cloth rippling wildly around its body, more active than normal.

Strangely, I did not react with fear. I just sat there, watching calmly.

The figure turned to me, raised one arm slowly and motioned. Of its own volition, my body responded. I was in a different kind of dream now, the kind you glide through without control, seeing everything, but exacting no change on the circumstance.

The material around my body rippled and moved, having a life of its own. I was petite and then I was huge- that body builder four cells down, someone people wouldn't trifle with, someone who would bust a hundred knee caps for a second bowl of soupy, unappealing chow. That thought was a brief flash of my old self though, quickly flooded with the rinse cycle, quickly banished from my water-logged brain.

I was standing next to one of the hospital beds now, one that held a woman, her breasts large and flopping to the sides, her too-pale nipples resting in her somewhat chunky armpits. The figure didn't direct me; I knew to begin pushing the bed. It moved easily, set on four rollers. The silent figure held the door open for me and I continued walking and pushing. We moved through halls, my vision perfectly clear although I knew how dim the lights were in reality.

We ended our journey in a hot room filled with steam.

I moved the bed toward a second one that was empty. I left it there, feeling little for the exposed woman. My eyes roved the room, seeing through the haze. Two large cylinders rose from the ground; the fog was greatest here, billowing out from the openings of each circular housing.

Walking forward mechanically, I peered into what turned out to be reservoirs filled with boiling, opaque water. An oversized wooden ladle hung from a hook nearby. I retrieved it. Dipping the spoon into the water, I stirred, causing more steam to rise. After a moment, there was a pressure against my push and I knew I'd hit something solid in the hot liquid. I lifted the ladle toward the surface.

Water poured off of a large piece of paleness. A thigh. Boneless, skinless, human thigh. The other white meat.

Inside of me, the human remnant fought to release itself from the whitewater rapids coursing through my brain. The fight was short-lived as the furious waters in my mind drowned me.

Exploring the room again, I found a series of large blenders on a long table. Beside those, there were pots with metal serving utensils.

Something touched my shoulder.

I turned, unalarmed.

The figure that led me to this room held out one of the pots filled with khaki slop. I'd never heard one of them talk before. Not until now.

"Feeding time." The voice was feminine, but brisk. It was... somehow familiar.

Suddenly, the human was fighting again inside my mind. This time, she was strong enough to exact some force. She gave me a headache. I wanted her to shut up, to leave me alone. I didn't know her name, because she didn't matter. This was our body now, ours to control. No. It was her body? No. Our body.

Human. I was human.

My hand traveled upward, reached for the covering over the figure's face. It did not move, did not keep me from my purpose. My fingers grasped the smooth, dark material and I yanked with force, jerking the figure's head slightly forward.

At one time, I'd thought that monsters are never as scary once you can see their faces and call them by their names.

I'd been wrong.

"Aunt April?" The words escaped my lips, a rushed breathy utterance.

Then the human inside me was quelled again, the recognition of her face disappearing in an onslaught of mind-numbing rinse cycle. A little detergent, a little dish soap – all that was needed to cleanse away the human stain. Then I became 'figure' again; the body became 'ours' again, and I followed the other figure, whose face was once again covered, out of the kitchen and toward the prison. We each bore a full pot of *human* chow and a serving ladle.

About Eli Constant

Eli Constant is a genre-jumping detail junkie, obsessed with the nature of humanity. She believes that there is beauty at the core of most everything, but that truly unredeemable characters create the best stories. Eli is the author of "DEAD TREES", "Dead Trees 2", "MASTIC","DRAG.N", and is a contributor to the charity anthology"LET'S SCARE CANCER TO DEATH" (LSCtD: TW Brown, Editor | MayDecember Publications) | 100% sales proceeds go to the V Foundation, a leader in cancer research for the past twenty years).

These 2014 Anthologies will be available soon (All featuring stories by Eli): "State of Horror: New Jersey" (Charon Coin Press), "State of Horror: Illinois" (Charon Coin Press), & "Dark Carnival" (Pen & Muse Press).

Eli's works-in-progress include the final book in the Dead Trees Trilogy, a 3-author anthology exploring the psychosis of serial killers, the second companion novel to DRAG.N, and a zombie origins novel (this last work in progress comes as a huge surprise to Eli; she honestly thought she'd never write about zombies, but somehow, she fell down the zombie hole and couldn't crawl out, or rather, didn't want to crawl out).

*

While completing coursework at USC-L, Columbia College, TAMU-CC, and George Mason University, Eli enjoyed a varied course load, but finally settled on Biology and focused on a career in lab research. She spent time in Texas at Flour Bluff Shrimp Mariculture Lab and also spent time at NIH participating in an Animal Research Program in the Infectious Disease Dept. It took two years working in Histology/Pathology for her to realize she wanted to be a writer.

Eli lives in Virginia with her husband Damion, their two children (with their third on the way), and her rescue hound. Find out more at www.eliconstant.com and keep posted on upcoming publications. Also follow Eli on Twitter (@Author_EliC), Facebook, Wordpress, and Google+.

Morgan Garcia

Introduction to "Perishable" by Morgan Garcia

Morgan decided to write for 'Fading Hope' because it was a chance to be apart of something that has the opportunity to showcase the much darker side of her imagination. Not to mention being able to be named alongside extremely talented authors. The apocalypse intrigues her. It's the unknown of what society will do if the world were to suddenly collapse out of the everyday norm.

Perishable

My wedding is so vivid to me that I can almost relive the sensation I felt as I walked down the aisle. I was so nervous; not out of fear of making a mistake, but out of excitement that I was finally getting married to the man I love.

Our relationship wasn't perfect; we fought almost constantly. It wasn't fighting out of hatred for one another; we were fighting because that's what happenes when people from two different worlds try to combine them into one.

I shouldn't have held back my tears as I stood in front of my soon-to-be-husband on the alter. I should have let my ecstatic emotions free but I wanted to remain composed because nobody wants to see an erratic bride.

Once we were pronounced, it was so easy to fall into a cloud of happiness; a cloud which we floated on for the rest of the day. It was just the two of us, it didn't really matter who else was there.

It was great to share the day with others that we cared for – but this day, this day was about us and we milked every second of it.

I remember when we took our first selfie as a married couple and posted it to Facebook immediately. We also decided to change our relationship status to 'married'...because that's what really made it official. Hah!

I try hard every day to keep these memories alive; because I want to hold onto that happiness for as long as I can...

*

Blast after blast shot out from the Walther PK380 as Suzanne was slowly surrounded by ravenous beings. She would have been happy to use her machete--it wouldn't be first time, but with a horde already in front of her, there was no reason to keep quiet now. Not to mention she preferred to stay as far away from them as possible.

She had lasted this long, and wasn't about to go down just because she had been separated from her group. So she was separated. Who cares? She could survive on her own for a while!

Or at least that's what she told herself. Had to keep sane, after all. She wasn't even clear on how she got separated from her group, but knew where they were headed. She just needed to get through this horde first.

She reached down into the big pouch on her tactical vest where she stored all of her bullets. Her eyes widened and her heart skipped a beat as she realized that the pouch was now hauntingly empty.

"Oh fuck." She said aloud as she began to more closely survey her surroundings. She saw several openings and even though she knew it was most likely suicidal, she needed to make a run for it before they got close enough to start gnawing on her flesh.

As quickly as she could, she barreled through the horde, feeling their slimy hands grabbing at her, but focusing all her attention far into the distance, not really focusing in on anything in particular. She didn't dare to stop and kept running on as quickly as she was able. She knew they wouldn't be able to catch up to her, hoped they had already forgotten all about her.

She slowed and tried to breathe quietly, even though she desperately desired oxygen. She grabbed the hose which was connected to a CamelBak bladder that was tucked inside her backpack and took a swig of water.

Once she no longer felt like she was dying from lack of oxygen, she began searching through all of her pockets, hoping to at least find a couple of bullets to get her through to her next destination.

She could never hide her feelings well, even if there was no one around to see her. She swallowed hard as she leaned against a tree and holstered her gun.

She had her bow and that was going to have to do for the time being. She just hoped she wouldn't run into anyone – or anything - else.

She thought for a second then pulled out a map. The map was filled with scribbles, stains and wet spots, but somehow she was still able to read it. "Nancy's Nursing Home. Right on." She spoke softly to no one in particular. It was a common occurrence to talk out loud to herself, it was far more comforting than silence.

She stood up, did a quick body check of herself to make sure everything was still intact then proceeded forward. Nightfall was approaching and she knew she had to hustle to get to the nursing home.

When she arrived, surprisingly, there was still the same amount of security as when she first saw it so many months ago when the shit had first hit the fan. She had been forced into instructing the people how to take care of themselves and the facility because they were unwilling to move somewhere safer. Not that it was a shock, half of the residents could barely get out of bed, let alone hold a gun or even more demanding, fire the thing.

Suzanne saluted the men who were watching from the rooftop with rifles hugged tightly to their chests. They nodded to her as the door flung open to allow her entrance once they realized who she was and that she wasn't a threat.

The woman at the front desk looked up and her face instantly brightened when she saw who it was.

"Oh! Suzanne! It's so great to see you! She's been so worried about you."

"Hey, Becky. Had any luck convincing her to come with me?"

Becky shook her head with a goofy smile, "Oh no, dear. You know I wouldn't do that."

Suzanne glared and frowned, "Even though I asked you to? After everything I've done for this place, you couldn't do this one little thing?" Her tone was harsh, much harsher than it would have been in any other situation. Ever since the apocalypse began, her fuse had gotten shorter and shorter. She was lucky she had any self-control at all at this point.

Becky tilted her head, bit her tongue and turned the goofy smile into a sincere one, "I'm sorry, but I've told you before, these people wouldn't be able to survive out there. Isn't that why you helped us to become self-sustaining, to protect them from the outside world?"

Suzanne rolled her eyes and groaned, "My mom would be perfectly capable out there."

Becky smiled bigger, in her head reminding herself that she wouldn't be alive if it weren't for Suzanne, "You sure about that?" She looked down, "I know...I wouldn't be able to handle it."

Suzanne stared at her blankly for a moment then looked away, succumbing to the fact, yet again, that not everyone is cut out for cold blooded killing. She changed the subject, "Well, is she awake?"

Becky's voice turned chipper once more, "I think so! Head on back!" Becky said as she pulled out her keys, yanked on the giant lock attached to the chain-link fence and unlocked it, then pushed the door open slightly.

"Thanks." Suzanne didn't bother to push it open too much more, just squeezed through. She quickly progressed down the hallway, knowing exactly where she was going.

In no time, she was knocking on one of the doors, "Mom, it's me, Suzanne."

On the other side she heard a slight yet high pitched voice, "Suzanne? Is that really you? Or are you one of those creatures?"

"It's me, Mom. Those creatures don't have a high enough brain function to be able to not only speak, but to mimic my voice."

The door cracked open as a woman, who didn't look frail but merely old and rundown, peaked through the crack at Suzanne.

"Mom, if you think I'm one of them, why would you crack the door open to check? They'd just push themselves through." Suzanne replied as patiently as she could.

"Oh I know that!" She said as she whipped the door open fully. "I just didn't want one of the nurses to play a trick on me!"

Suzanne walked in, closed and locked the door behind her. "The nurses play tricks on you?"

"Well...it's more of a game we all play." She sat down on her bed.

Suzanne smirked as she walked directly to the dresser, opened the top drawer and began pulling out several guns. "Yes! He hasn't been here yet." She said with elation.

"Who hasn't been here? Your brother? Allen? No, he hasn't. He never visits me. Ungrateful little..."

"He's surviving too, you know." Suzanne replied in defense of her brother.

"He's got a bad kidney!"

"No, Mom, his kidney is fine, thanks to your generous donation."

Her mother grumbled. "Yeah, he's running around with my kidney and he can't even come and visit me!"

Suzanne walked to the closet and began pulling out a couple shotguns. "He's going to be pissed when he sees all his guns have gone missing." She whispered to herself then chuckled slyly. She then pushed a box aside to reveal an AR-15; she had needed a rifle, sometimes a handgun just wasn't enough. She took a deep breath in as if it were love at first sight. She smiled and almost had to wipe a tear away as she pulled it out and stroked it. "Hello, beautiful."

She had assembled the AR herself many months prior to the apocalypse, with her husband's helped. She had to leave it behind until things calmed down as she needed to focus on carrying only a few weapons at a time. It was lightweight but she had other priorities at the time and had to make compromises, and instead took more manageable items such as knives and handguns.

She attached the shotguns to her backpack as best as she could using extra MOLLE straps. She slung her AR over her shoulder then secured the pistols in her coat and vest pockets.

She walked back to the dresser and began emptying ammo into her vest pockets. She was starting to feel like a pack mule, but she would never complain; staying alive was her top priority.

Her mother blurted, "Have you found him yet?"

Suzanne stopped with her hands in her pockets, took a deep breath and licked her lips, "I stayed there as long as I could. The house was compromised. Not to mention I was running out of food. And the rest of the team was waiting for me." Her eyes welled up even though she was trying her damndest to hold back tears, "I had to go."

"You haven't heard from him at all?" Her mother sounded shocked.

"Mom, he was a day away from returning home from London when Hell broke loose. He's...he's not coming back." She continued to pile the rest of the ammo in her pouches, wiping away a stray tear. She whispered, almost to herself, "I'm sure he's still alive. I just...probably won't ever see him again." She turned around and forced a half smile, "So you stayin' or comin'?'"

"Staying." her mom replied without hesitation, "I've gotten pretty comfortable around here. I'm sewing more than usual, still have reruns of Project Runway to get me through...I'm good here." She really was ok with her way of life.

Suzanne smiled softly, "Sounds great." There was a small awkward silence as Suzanne contemplated staying with her. It wouldn't be so bad, she'd be able to take shifts staying on guard, helping with the garden, building some more solar panels...

But that wasn't her mission. She couldn't just sit around at a retirement home and wait for the apocalypse to end. She had to fight. She had to survive.

She *had* to keep busy to keep her mind off the fact that she was probably never going to see her husband again.

Suzanne threw on her backpack and immediately her knees trembled with the extra weight she had accumulated from the guns and ammo. "Oof. This is not a good idea."

"What? You leaving? Damn straight it's not a good idea." Her mother snapped.

"No, Mom, it's just a bit heavy. I'll be ok." She chuckled, "This one time, Jake and I were going camping and we had to hike two miles to get to our camp site. We each had these packs on our back filled with everything and the kitchen sink," she tightened the straps from her bag around her waist as she spoke, "and the trip there was awful because we were carrying way more than we should have, but the trip back for some reason was even worse!

"Knees were trembling, we were gasping for air, I even fell down and tore open my favorite pair of jeans." She laughed, "We were insane to pack all that stuff for one night!"

Suzanne stared down at the floor, her eyes blurred, and her smile faded into nothing. Audio of their last conversation echoed through her mind. She had called Jake the moment she saw the news reports, angry mobs, sick people filling hospitals. They had been preparing for a catastrophe like this for years so she knew how to distinguish the real signs from the fake. She remembered feeling numb when she heard Jake tell her, *they're shutting down the airports*. They were barely able to say that they loved each other before the call was disconnected. She had desperately tried to reconnect with him while barricading herself inside their safe room.

She even tried to text and even though a couple of them had gone through, she never received a reply back.

She kept her cell phone with her at all times and kept it charged with the solar panel that she carried on the outside of her backpack. She turned it on once a day, hoping that by some freak chance, there would be cell reception again. And that somehow, Jake would get back in contact with her and let her know that he was alive. That he was...okay.

Suzanne swallowed hard, holding her tears back once again. As she continued to stare at the ground, she said, "I've gotta go." Then she exhaled, looked up to her mother, stumbled over and hugged her, kissed her, said, "I love you, Mom," Then Suzanne left the room quickly, not wanting her or her mother to get upset with a long goodbye.

She strutted down the hallway with a new sense of urgency. Life was a lot harder without her husband, but she wasn't afraid to keep moving forward, even in the midst of uncertainty. She was letting her heart take control, something she always said not to do. She was fighting and surviving; but it just wouldn't be the same without Jake back in her life.

*

It had been three days since she left the retirement home, she had found an abandoned beer factory to call home for a few nights. Unfortunately there wasn't any beer tucked away in obscure corners, but it was clear of people, animals and other *things*, and that was good enough for her.

She wouldn't have stayed there so long except for the fact that every time she packed up to leave, it began pouring outside. It was getting on her nerves. Every day she wasted there was a day further from finding her team. She was sitting in the shadows in a corner, facing the main front entrance, which she had come in through. It seemed to be the only unchained door, so someone had to of been there before her and she hoped they wouldn't come back. The AR-15 was strewn over her lap, ready to be used at a moment's notice, as she stared at the door with a deadpan expression.

She was tired. She struggled to keep her eyes open. Her head and body kept trying to droop over into sweet unconsciousness but she wasn't about to fall asleep just to wake up to a group of people robbing her; most likely raping and then killing her.

Ironically, the quiet was what snapped her to her feet. The hypnotizing noise of the rain had finally dissipated, replaced with a constant dripping from the roof and chirping birds. She grinned and quickly packed her things.

She was quick to pack and pile everything on. She was sick of canned tuna, she had to catch a rabbit or squirrel or some kind of fresh meat soon. She took a moment to change the 55.6 bolt out of her AR-15 to a .22 bolt to not only make her hunting quieter, but a 55.6 bullet against small game was a tad overkill. Plus, she had way more .22 rounds than 55.6 so it wouldn't be an issue.

As she switched them out, she couldn't help but flash back in her mind to the Christmas that she gave the .22 bolt conversion kit to her husband. At the time, they were living together and waiting for the right time to get hitched.

He hadn't expected her to get him the conversion kit, even he thought it was too expensive. Which was ironic, because for that same Christmas he had bought the rest of the parts needed to finish building her AR-15, which amounted to much more than that conversion kit.

The memory vanished as she snapped the AR-15 closed with the .22 bolt inside and rested it to her side. She slowly made her way outside, making sure to examine every inch that she could see and tried to listen as best as she could, with her AR-15 up front and center, waiting for someone to try to come at her.

As she rounded the corner, she heard a noise. It sounded like a bird pecking at something, or it could have been a small animal; couldn't be sure yet. She paused, even held her breath and waited for the noise again. If it was an animal, she had to be prepared to act quickly in order to kill it for a fresh meal.

She had stood there for only a few moments when she heard the sound again. But it didn't sound like breaking twigs or a bird pecking like she had originally thought; it sounded like...

It dawned on her. She lowered her weapon, reached down to her left front breast pocket and pulled out her cell phone. She frowned, suspecting that it was just low on battery and beeping at her. She shook her head, trying to remember when she had turned it off of vibrate mode. When silence meant life or death in this apocalyptic world, she never would have dreamed of putting her phone on ringer mode.

She pressed the power button on top and it took her no time to realize what was on her screen. She stopped breathing when she saw two text messages. Both from her husband.

She quickly swiped to unlock her phone and read the text messages.

The first read, "*There's a boat going to the US. I'm on it. I'll be there soon.*"

The second read, "*I love you.*"

The time stamp read 36 days ago.

Her lips parted from shock as tears began to well up in her wide eyes. Her heart pounded and she took shallow, slow breaths, trying to hold back tears. She knew she had to keep moving forward. These texts meant that...she didn't even care how she suddenly received them...they meant that...that...

She blinked and when her eyes refocused on, she saw a shattered screen and heard the echo of a gunshot. It was as if she had lost moments of time, as if she were literally lost in her own thoughts of finally being reunited with the love of her life.

She blinked swiftly a couple times then began to feel pain in her chest. Her eyes squinted, jaw clenched and she could feel a thick, wet sensation against her chest.

She slowly lifted her head to see blurry shapes of people in the distance. Deep down, she wanted to reach for her weapon and retaliate, but between the pain in her chest and her mind racing with thoughts of never being reunited with her husband again - not to mention the gun shot wound in her chest - she was paralyzed.

Blood dripped out the corner of her mouth.

Her eyes crossed.

The last tears she would ever shed rolled down her cheeks.

She crumbled to the ground.

She was able to focus on her phone, which had landed half a foot in front of her.

She could feel her heart slow, as she tried to will her hand to reach her phone in order to send one last text message to her husband.

Soon, everything around her deafened and darkened.

Her mind and body finally calmed as she exhaled for the last time, she was able to vividly picture the moment they kissed, after being pronounced as man and wife.

About Morgan Garcia

Morgan is a modern survivalist who preps for emergencies and disasters on a regular basis. Writing about apocalyptic scenarios has been a bi-product of being a prepper. When she isn't prepping or writing, she is doing any number of activities, including, but not limited to; voice acting, riding her motorcycle or doing the suburban housewife thing with her husband and two beagle mixes.

Thea Gregory

Introduction to "Radio Silence" by Thea Gregory

Radio Silence emerged out of the slush pile for the Zombie Bedtime Stories. It was cut not for quality, but because it was a stand-alone story marooned in a complex, non-linear series. I loved the concept of betrayal and wanted to further explore the self-destructive nature of humanity. I enjoy writing about atypical protagonists—an old man seemed like a great way to break out of my comfort zone and imagine someone very different than most zombie story characters. Most of all, I've always wanted to imply mystery meat. There, the real truth comes out!

Radio Silence

Michael pulled the clock key from around his neck, its tarnished brass a dull green in the candle's flickering light. The thin leather cord that tied it around his neck dangled limply from the keyhole, its frayed edges caressing the metal. Smoke from the old wood stove tickled his nose, and he sucked in a deep breath and held it as he let the stillness of the world settle into him. For six months, he'd maintained the ritual of keeping time. Years before, he'd wound his uncle's clock out of duty and obligation. Now, it was different obligation that spurred him forward. A need for order.

He exhaled as his thick, veiny fingers slid the key into the hole on the front of the antique clock, an heirloom inherited from his long-dead uncle. Rich varnish meshed with the cast iron moldings, peaking in knotted wood carving forgotten by modern designers. By some miracle, he'd been able to turn off the chime without damaging the myriad spinning gears and levers inside. He couldn't let them hear.

Sucking in another breath, he turned the key clockwise, listening intently to the sounds outside the room as he twisted. Everyone upstairs was still asleep—the next watch wouldn't start for another hour.

He twisted the key again and again, until at last the clock was wound. "That's another month we've got," Michael muttered under his breath. The rest remained unsaid: If we're not dead first.

He replaced the key around his neck, tucking it beneath the lapels of his plaid flannel shirt. Michael then turned to face the room, his ritual completed. His small cottage—his sanctuary-turned-prison had seen better days. Dated wood paneling covered the walls, floors, and ceilings. The windows were blocked by an assortment of bedding, burlap sacks, and even cobbled together plastic shopping bags. A tear came to his eye when his gaze came to the solid wooden bookshelves—his vaunted collection of literature. The shelves were now packed with whatever food they could find. The books were nothing more than a memory of warmth on a cold winter's morning. Michael longed to curl up in his bed and let a classic take him to another time, or escape with something modern. But now, all he had to read were food tins and radio manuals.

Michael shook his head, and the memories of happier days and good books dissipated. He walked over to the sink, and smiled as water once again greeted him.

Gratified that his years of resisting upgrading the cottage's well had turned out for the best, he filled a pot of water and set it on the wood stove.

Jacob wasn't any good to anyone before he'd had his morning coffee. Of course, coffee was just a memory now, unless they had a lucky scavenging run. But, it seemed that dried chicory root or tea would do in a pinch.

Michael's neck turned at the sound of gentle footfalls coming from above. He stretched and rolled his shoulders, pushing his hands into the aura of warmth surrounding the wood stove.

"Hey, old man," said a deep voice held just above a whisper. "Where's my damn coffee?"

Michael turned and nodded at the young man, just shy of twenty five. His dark eyes latched onto Michael's, and flashed him a predatory grin, teeth white against the beginnings of a patchy beard.

Jacob was among the youngest of their band of survivors, but Michael knew him to be as calm and controlled as any elder. "Coming right up," he replied in a hushed voice.

Jacob crossed from the stairs to the kitchen and took down his favorite mug—an old souvenir from Alcatraz. Michael had visited over a decade ago, and brought the mug back to the cabin as a souvenir. Now, Jacob refused to use any other cup. He then glided over to the empty bookshelf and retrieved a yellow tin.

Jacob turned and examined the just-steaming pot of water. He pursed his lips as he spooned a crumbly brown substance into the cup. "Looks like Priss and I need to go do some shopping," he said.

Michael rubbed his forehead with the back of his hand, and shivered. "It's not too soon?" he asked, leaving out the end of the question: After we lost Suzanne. That had been a productive raid, but where three had left, only two returned.

Jacob chortled and hefted the pot off the stove just as the bubbles began to break the surface. "Doesn't matter if it's too soon or not, old man," he said as he swirled the murky contents of the cup.

"Grass grows, birds shit, and I need a decent fucking cup of coffee." He sniffed the contents of the cup and scrunched up his face.

Michael shook his head and sighed.

Jacob took a swig of the homebrew and grimaced. "Yup. That settles it. We're totally going to visit Wayne Jones' farmhouse. If I have to drink this shit, I'm going to eat good meat."

"You don't mean the pig farmer's, do you?" Michael asked. He'd talked to Wayne over the CB radio, until the power went out and the generator's ensuing power surge had fried the unit. Jacob and Priss had visited his farm soon after, but without the proper supplies and technical know-how, the radio would never work again.

"Yeah, why not? Bonus if the old fart's still alive, but..." Jacob paused to take another gulp of his drink, "But, ya' know, free pork either way, right?"

Michael nodded. Their last visit to Wayne's had resulted in some fifty pounds of salted and desiccated meat, just after the radio had failed. The thought of a good slab of meat made him salivate. "You can't be taking him for granted, Jacob," he said, before shaking his head, "but, I won't say no to free meat."

"I knew you'd come around," Jacob said. He chugged the rest of his drink in one fluid motion, and wiped his mouth with the back of his hand. "So, I'm thinking that me and Priss will set out at dawn, tomorrow. We gotta get our things together. It's about a three hour walk out to Wayne's digs, and four back if he sends us loaded up."

"You're not taking the main roads, are you?" Michael asked. That was how they'd lost Suzanne, and the others.

"Not this time," Jacob said, setting his cup down on the wooden kitchen table. "I think we've learned better than to take the easy way. Buggers don't like to be alone in the woods."

"Okay, fine. I'll make sure you've got provisions for the day during my watch." Michael rubbed his eyes, trying to massage away the dull ache building in his sinuses. Getting old sucked. Getting old in a dusty cabin with no good food sucked even more.

"Sounds good to me. Thanks, old man." Jacob mock-saluted and then dropped down into the kitchen chair, swinging his feet up onto the table. "Now, get your ass to bed before it gets cold."

Michael touched two fingers to his brow and moved towards the worn wooden steps. His hand seized the banister and he hauled himself upwards, one step at a time. The air cooled with every step away from the wood stove. He opened the first door on the right and tip-toed over the sleeping forms huddled on the floor, until he reached the bed. Dropping into the still-warm embrace of the blankets, he closed his eyes and allowed sleep to wash over him.

There was blood everywhere. Limbs spurting gouts of blood. Blood become raindrops and pattering on the ground. It was on Michael's hands, working itself into the aged grooves of his skin. His nails were black and clotted with it. The smell of copper stung his nose and worked its way into his mouth. Saliva and bile gushed forward, but not before the screams started.

Michael sat bolt upright in his tiny cot, his skin beading with cold sweat. The dreams of before the cataclysm that had torn the world into little pieces always ended with the screams. At first, they were his friends' screams, as distinct and unique as each of them had been. But, as time marched on, their voices had melted into a singular dread chorus.

He checked his hands, quickly, just to be sure. They were clean of blood. But, the memory of his labors over their lifeless forms persisted. A tourniquet sealing the raw meat of a severed limb. Pressure on a seeping bite wound. One by one, they'd dropped into a deep sleep... followed by the nothingness of a temporary death.

Michael shut his eyes, and sucked in a deep breath. He forced the air from his lungs, before dragging in another deep inhalation. He clenched his teeth. No, I will *not* remember this, he thought. But, their pale forms still swung listlessly in the eternal focus of his mind's eye.

He swung one leg over the side of the bed, then another. His back and his hips expressed their typical geriatric neediness. He dismissed them, with more success than he'd had vanquishing the ghosts of his fallen comrades.

He might not be able to help them, not after all this time. His friends were likely still out there in the woods, lost and alone. Lost and screaming. But, he knew he could get Wayne's radio working again.

Wayne's voice wouldn't be warped into screams. Not like them.

Not like them, memory whispered in agreement.

Michael pulled himself to the small chest of drawers his father had made as a youth. His shaking hands reached towards the unfinished, wooden drawers, quiet and determined. Silence was a skill to be embraced. It let the sleepers continue with their rest, and it kept the others from finding them during the long nights. Michael never thought he'd be nostalgic for the pervasive light pollution that had plagued this portion of the continent. At least you could see. The stars were cold comfort when they shrouded fiends.

He drew out some clothes—a faded plaid jacket and a ragged pair of jeans. Michael turned them over as he changed so he wouldn't see the stain that still graced the backside of the pants. That was all he had left of Sharon. Or, was it his precious Jillian? That fateful evening was still a blur, further obscured by the fog of time. His trembling hands withdrew a faded army green knapsack, its narrow armbands frayed and coated in the grime of his juvenile handprints. He discarded his worn clothes in a heap at the foot of the bed. Someone on cleaning duty would tend to them later.

Michael straightened, rolling his shoulder back until a pop could be heard. The relief was short lived, however. He looked back for a moment before making his way down the old staircase.

Sunlight crept through the cracks in the blinds, fingers of light caressing furniture and illuminating the particles of dust that floated through the air. A deep inhale unsettled the dust, sending it swirling through the room. The kitchen was devoid of life—Jacob had likely started his morning squirrel hunt and the early risers were usually in the garden.

Michael moved to the desk in the corner, and sat down in front of his faithful radio. Its once bright polish was now tarnished, and long hours had worn finger imprints into the controls.

He settled the familiar headphones over his ears and flicked it on, the hum reassuring him that his last connection to the outside world still operated. His fingers danced over dials as he went through the motions of scanning through the frequencies, searching for word on other survivors. At last, he tuned in to Wayne's preferred frequency, and waited.

Leaving the headphones on, he opened a drawer. Often on his long nights alone, he thought of every possible malfunction that could knock out a radio. Michael didn't have a spare antenna, but he was sure that he had spares of just about every other part. He'd made sure to visit electronics stores during the first few raids they'd made on the city, before the Army had begun exterminating civilians and looting the stores themselves. Now, it was too risky to leave the country retreat and they'd been forced to improvise. Michael had listened to the carnage as an invisible spectator—bearing witness to the end of freedom, decency, and human life. Even Jacob understood that the city was off-limits until the marauders moved on.

Michael's hands moved from part to part. He checked the connections to be sure they were free of corrosion and packed them into a small plastic tackle box he's repurposed for storing electronics.

The red box had a handle, but was small enough to easily fit into his knapsack. Perspiration stuck to his brow and moistened the limp remains of his once proud head of hair.

He sniffed and pursed his lips as he finished packing the colorful little parts and wires into their container. Then, he rummaged around the bottom of the drawer until he withdrew a soldering iron, some solder, and one of his precious remaining packs of batteries. His fingers hesitated for a moment before dropping the latter into the bag. Then, he tucked the tackle box in on top of it and stood up. For an instant, his fingers curled around the key dangling from his neck. The leather dug into the skin of his neck and the metal was warm against the palm of his hand. For a moment, he wondered what his uncle would have done. But, he shook his head and dismissed the thought. His uncle would have kept the clock running, not go off on a crazy mission to fix a radio.

Michael sighed. He slung the backpack over his shoulder and turned towards the front porch. He could at least enjoy the afternoon sunlight while he waited for Jacob to get back. His bones creaked their agreement and he plodded towards the door.

Michael took a deep breath, his nostrils flaring against the morning air. Still laden with dew, it carried to him smells of rotting leaves and fresh pine. He squinted at the distance, forcing the trail into focus. Dampness clung to him like a second skin, but he didn't complain. At least he had been allowed to come along —to be useful.

They had been walking in silence for what seemed like hours. His leg creaked as he stepped over yet another fallen tree. Mud clung to his worn boots. He raised a hand to swat a mosquito when something caught his eye in the distance. Something grey—about the size of a man, but wasted and lean.

His feet stuck to the ground, as though his muscles couldn't decide if they wanted to freeze him into a statue or send him flying into the woods like a doe. It rustled in the trees behind him. He spun in a fluid motion that belied his age to face it. His eyes widened as memory flooded his reality with images of Jillian, her leg ripped from the cradle of its socket, crawling towards him. Her large blue eyes pleaded for him to make her whole again. Thick brown hair tattered and out of place. Calling his name—calling for the father who couldn't save her.

A hand clapped against his back, and he jumped. Heart racing and blood pounding through his ears, he turned. Jacob squinted at him, before shaking his head. Priss—a young woman with stringy hair and a tattered nostril which had once held a nose ring rolled her eyes and turned away. A scowl had been etched on her face for as long as he'd known her, drawing harsh lines on her supple skin. Something about Priss made his skin crawl.

"Shit, old timer," Jacob said in a low voice, shaking his head. "At least we know your hearing is still good!"

"Shh!" Priss growled, her eyes narrowing into slits.

"Whatever, Priss. It's a fucking squirrel." Jacob took Michael by the crook of the elbow and led him further down the path before continuing. "I don't know why I put up with that woman. Freaks out over squirrels and fucking gets me into all kinds of trouble. You know what I mean, Mikey?"

Michael only shook his head. He looked back to where he'd seen the figure, but the trees had moved. He raised a trembling hand to point to where it used to be. He drew in breath after rattling breath, but only the sound of the desperate rushing of his own blood reached his ears.

Jacob peered back in the direction of Michael's outstretched finger. His head cocked and his eyes narrowed. "Priss!" he hissed in little more than a whisper as he hefted the solid stick he carried into both hands.

Priss glared at him, the grimace turning her features to stone.

A screeching howl cut through the air. Michael's heart skipped a beat, and renewed memories of blood and gore played through his mind. It was one of them! A fiend—one of the formerly human inhabitants of this valley—had found their safe trail!

"Run!" Jacob shoved Michael down the trail with a force that threatened to bring the old man to his knees.

Michael recovered, and sprinted down the trail. His knapsack bounced as he ran, the heavy tackle box smacking into his aching lower back. He shot past trees and over mud puddles in his mad dash away from it. Another soulless scream shattered the tranquility of the forest path.

Footsteps sounded behind him. Michael grit his teeth and drove himself further, faster than he'd gone even as a young man playing soccer. He drew in ragged breaths and his legs wobbled, but he maintained the pace.

They turned around a bend in the trail and there it was—Wayne's farmhouse. The gate hung ajar, and the grey wooden fence had collapsed in many places. The grass was overgrown and no smoke curled from the chimney.

Michael found himself slowing, until another scream spurred him forward again. Jacob said, between pants: "Get inside!"

Pain shot through Michael's feet as he pushed himself through the dilapidated gate. He glanced backwards. An emaciated man—or, what had been a man once—was chasing them. His grey skin was stretched over his bones, and most of his hair had fallen out. A gash in his scalp displayed an arch of sun bleached bone. Michael screamed, his breath hot and metallic, and put on one final burst of speed.

The door fell off the hinges as he barreled through it, so he took shelter in the next room. Jacob stopped and readied the heavy stick. Priss had drawn a rusty old machete from her pack. Jacob took a step forward, bellowing as his staff connected with the thing's head. Paper-thin skin split open, and its face sloughed down over its chest as the living corpse tumbled to the ground.

Priss stepped forward with the nimbleness of a dancer, bringing the heavy blade over the thing's neck in one fell swoop.

It was over. Michael took a deep, shaking breath. His whole body shook. He took an uneven step towards the front door when his left foot hit something and sent it clattering across the wooden floor. His eyes traced its motion. It was off-white with defined hard edges. A glance around the room showed that something had happened here. The furniture was not as he remembered it. It was stained with water, or perhaps something else? Isolation could do funny things to people. He walked after the spinning object, and gasped.

It was a chunk of bone. But why was there bone in the house? Wayne wasn't the type to bring his work home with him. Squatting, he picked it up. He spun it through his shaking fingers, peering at the smoothness of the break. The roughness of its core scraped against his weathered skin. He let it fall to the floor.

"You home, Wayne?" he called out. His voice wheezed.

After waiting a few moments for a reply, he glanced back at the door. He then drew off his backpack, and fumbled with the handle of his tackle box before pulling it free. If memory served, the radio was in the kitchen. He picked his way past a shattered coffee table.

His eyes scanned the walls and windows. The wallpaper was faded, its vertical stripes marred by cracks and scuffs. He paused mid-step, and listened. Jacob was cursing somewhere in the distance. There were no other sounds other than the rustle of leaves and Michael's heaving breaths. He shrugged. Perhaps Wayne was in the barn, tending to his small army of hogs.

He crossed the threshold into the kitchen, and he let his eyes scan the room as he bent over, hands on his aching knees. A dank musk assailed his nostrils. Sweat clung to his eyelids. Michael tried to rub the moisture from his brow with the back of his hand, but he only succeeded in getting the salty liquid into his eyes.

Blinking, he focused on a wooden school desk in the corner, next to the counter. The counter was covered in plastic bins, each heaped high with salt. His stomach grumbled at the suggestion of food, but he ignored it—there was time for a snack later.

He pulled the worn office chair back from the desk, his fingers melding into the exposed yellow padding. He placed the tackle box on the chair's cracked fabric seat before examining the radio. When he flipped the power switch, the lights winked to life.

He pursed his lips, and began turning the dials. All seemed to be in order. He shook his head, and he stretched over the radio, peering behind it. His shaking fingers traced each wire to its proper connection. Michael's grasping reached the sharp cut of metal. He gasped and pulled his hand back, staring at the droplet of blood that had welled up on his right index finger.

The injured finger went into his mouth. He grimaced at the coppery taste as he sucked. Why would the wire be cut? He squatted down, and squinted under the desk. Underneath, two wires lay on the floor. Their twisted copper innards were cut, creating a nest of metal.

Michael tried to stand. He gulped down air, the contents of his stomach churning against gravity. His eyes caught another glint of white, and he cried out. A pair of human skulls, broken and missing the jaws, sat under the kitchen table.

Michael's legs collapsed out from under him, and he landed on his tailbone, hard. One of the skulls was completely cleaned of flesh, while the other had some tendrils of gore still clinging to it. His eyes widened.

Footsteps echoed behind him. "I was hoping you wouldn't see this, old man," Jacob said.

Michael's mouth was too tired to articulate more than one word. "Why?"

"Well, y'see, humans are edible too. That fucker wouldn't give us meat, so we put in a change of ownership."

Bile rose to Michael's mouth. His eyes spun around, and rested on the pristine radio sitting in the corner of the room.

A sharp pain connected with the back of Michael's head. Blackness followed. The last thing he heard was Jillian's voice. *Daddy?*

About Thea Gregory

Thea Gregory is a girl with a physics degree. She loves the dark edges that caress the silver lining of life. Her passions are science fiction, the human condition, and anything that challenges our humanity. Thea loves running, pushups, cooking, and has been known to crochet a thing or two. She has a weakness for gaming and Star Trek. Thea is the author of the Zombie Bedtime Stories, and The ABACUS Protocol. She lives in Montreal with her two cats.

Claire C. Riley

Introduction to "Honey-Bee", by Claire C. Riley

When I sat down to write Honey-Bee I didn't have some great plan that I was intending to follow, nor did I have an idea on storyline. I just sat in front of my keyboard and let the words come to me.

The way I write is to picture an image, and from that image words spew forth, and a world evolves. I didn't know where it was going when I started, or what was going to happen, it was as big a mystery to me as it will be to you.

I imagined a woman sat on the bonnet of her car smoking a cigarette. The smoke circling her face as hunger pangs crippled her, and worry ran through her veins. She wants to give up, but knows she can't—not yet. Her thoughts are that of regret as she reminisced about the past and the mistakes that not just her, but humanity as a whole made, so many things we took for granted.

But, you know, she can probably tell you better than I can what this story is about...

Life ends.

No matter who you are, life always ends.

You are not important anymore. Who you are, nor who you were. You are simply food for the clawing, red-eyed monsters, with teeth like knives.

They will hunt you out, no matter where you seek shelter. In the light, in the dark, the monsters, they always come.

We all have them within us, and even with the small glimpse of beauty that is my yellow haired Lilly, I know that we shall not outlive this horror.

Because life ends. Life will always end.

No matter who you are, no matter where you hide.

For there is no hiding from the monster within.

Even for my sweet Lilly and I.

Honey-Bee

One.

There are times when I wish for the old days. For bills, and jobs, and too much TV. For fast food, sports cars, and thoughts about the ozone layer and how we can repair it.

Now we know that there was never any way to repair it. That it didn't matter how high your cholesterol was in the end, because you would die a slow and agonizing death anyway. Or maybe you would go quickly. Regardless, you would die.

So what would I say if I could go back in time and speak to the old me? Or even the old you? I'd say this: Get fat—eat the food you love, because soon enough it will be gone; love freely, and hate with regret; drive fast, but be mindful of others on the road because one day in the not-so-distant future, you might need those people to save you.

I would tell you not to waste too much of your time pondering what to do with your life, and just enjoy the here and now as much as you can. Because before you know it, it will be too late. Doctor, lawyer, farmer, computer technician, police officer, delivery driver—in this world that I live in now, none of that matters. Who you were isn't important anymore; it's who you are now that is significant.

I look out across the ocean with a sigh; the waves gently caressing the pebbled beach, reminding me of happier times.

"Mama?"

I turn to look at Lilly through the windshield of the car and offer her a small smile. Her little hands, as usual, are clasping her teddy bear with all their might. Her wide brown eyes stare back at me in confusion until at last recognition crosses her face and she seems satisfied with who I am, and that I am not far from her side. She knows that I am not her mother, but I am all she has now. She closes those brown pools of innocence again and snuggles back down into her car seat. She should know by now that I am never far from her side. She is mine, and I am hers. It has been this way since we found each other.

I slide off the hood of my car, take one last drag of my cigarette, and stub it out into the ground with a shake of my head. I swore I'd never smoke again. That's another thing to add to the list: if you want to smoke, do it. But be aware that when they run out—the cigarettes—it's a real bitch, and there's no running to the store to get more.

I walk to the edge of the cliff to get a better view of down below. The sun is just setting over the ocean, creating a myriad of colorful beauty before my eyes. It's easy to believe that everything is okay when I am up here. I can pretend there's nothing to be afraid of—no boogeyman hiding under the bed, no evil in the world. Just Lilly, the ocean, and me.

I jump when Lilly's hand clasps mine. Looking down into her sad face, I try to force a smile.

"You should be sleeping, my little Honey-Bee," I say as I squeeze her tiny hand gently.

She continues to stare blankly at me until I reach down and pull her up into my arms. She doesn't resist, but clings to me like a little koala bear. That thought makes me sadder still. She will never know what a koala bear is. They are all gone now, along with almost every other beautiful thing that once existed in this world.

I stare up at the stars, my heart feeling heavier than usual. Damn, they look beautiful tonight. Like tiny diamonds sprinkled across a black canvas. Lilly's hand tips my chin down so that I am looking at her again.

"Where are they?" she asks.

"Down there, Honey-Bee," I say, pointing to down below.

She peers over as much as she dares, her tiny fingers digging into my skin as she watches the abominations below. I feel her little body shiver and tense in my arms.

"It's okay. We are up here, and they are down there. We are safe," I reassure her. "We have our light still." I point to the streetlight, which inexplicably is still lit after all this time. It makes no sense, but I've given up trying to fathom it out. I'm just grateful it is.

"For now," she whispers. Her words cut into my heart, and I nod.

"Yes. For now, for tonight. And that is what matters. Tonight we can dance under the stars, Honey-Bee." I smile and twirl her around in circles, and she giggles. It is the sweetest sound I have heard in a long time—much better than the time we found the little gray kitten hiding under the burnt out car, crying out for its mother.

And even better than the sound of the breeze moving through the long grass and flowers in the field that I found Lilly hiding in—though that is a very close second. My little Honey-Bee, hiding in the sunflower field. I thought it was the most beautiful thing I had ever seen, as if God had shone His light upon that particular field. In the middle of a world filled with so much loss—so much death—how could there possibly be so much beauty? Then I saw her little face, peering up at me surrounded by yellows, oranges, and greens of the sunflowers. She was like a gift to me. I was so close to losing it, and then she—Lilly—was there, her face a more beautiful canvas than the sunflower field.

We wept in each other's arms that day, so happy to have found one another. Lilly and I dance until the sky further darkens and the stars seem to multiply, though she does not ever let me put her down. She grows heavy in my arms, and her eyelids begin to flutter closed again. I take her back to the car and place her in the little seat, clipping her in safely, being careful not to wake her up. I learned my lesson of not buckling her in when she sleeps and having to make a hasty retreat. She suffered a bump to her head that day, and I still feel guilty about it.

I light up another cigarette as I shut the door on her sleeping form, and go to stand at the edge again, looking down at them.

They gurgle and hiss, their red eyes staring back up at me. The sounds of their jagged nails scrambling for placement on the side of the cliff worries me, but they cannot climb. We are safe. For tonight, at least, thank God we are safe.

*

Light peeks over the top of the hillside, glaring in at me through the windshield. I rub my eyes and slouch further down in my seat, but the sun retaliates and rises further in the sky, making me groan and fully awaken.

"All right, all right," I mumble to myself.

I turn in my seat and see Lilly still sleeping, her little thumb tucked into her pink little rosebud mouth. My mouth twitches into what could possibly be considered a smile, but then I surrender myself to my misery again. I open the door and get out, taking my smokes out of my back pocket and lighting one up before I've even shut the door behind me.

The first wave of nicotine hits me and I relish the pleasure it brings me. There are only three things that bring me pleasure these days: Lilly, my cigarettes, and food. I walk to the edge and look down the cliff face, knowing that the monsters won't be there now—they are never there during the day. The night is their only friend.

Their previous night's antics are there to see, unfortunately, in the form of a bloodied pebbled beach and mutilated carcasses. I don't look close enough to see if they are human or animal bones. It doesn't matter—dead is dead, no matter what it is. I can't do anything about it. I finish my cigarette, feeling the hunger pangs subside a little, and go to the trunk of my car and open it to check our supplies. I know we are running low on everything, and if we don't find food soon, we will run out and starve.

I can survive without food longer than Lilly can, but it's been days now and I can feel myself growing weaker. The cigarettes were a great find to curb the hunger pangs, but even I'm going to need real food soon.

I pull out the last of the canned food: a small can of pinto beans. She hates pinto beans, and I hate the effort of having to make a fire to cook them on.

I was so pleased the day we found the stash of cans, so pleased. But now, as I stare at the last can, I think the beans were a curse, because we haven't found food since that day. I throw the can to the ground in anger, and slam the lid down on the trunk with a small sob. When I look up through the window, Lilly is staring back at me. Her wide brown eyes look frightened and I turn my sad face to a happy one for her, beckoning her out of the car to stretch her legs.

I pick her up as she climbs out, giving her a quick squeeze and a kiss on her forehead before pushing the soft curls back from her face.

"Morning, Honey-Bee."

"Morning."

"Did you sleep well?"

She nods. "I need to pee, bad." She bites on her bottom lip, a small frown furrowing her brow.

"Okay, let's go pee together." I smile and put her down, taking her hand as we walk away from the car and towards a bush. She stops as we near it. I turn to look at her.

"Check it," she pleads.

It's my turn to nod as I pull out my knife, release her hand, and walk the rest of the way to the bush on my own. I know there is nothing in there. She knows it too—the monsters only come out at night, and this bush isn't dense enough for them to hide in—but I play along. I always play along if it makes her feel better.

I slash into the bush with my knife. "Better come out, monsters. Lilly has to pee real bad." I turn and watch as her sweet features soften into a smile. "If there's any of you in here, you better move along or you're gonna get it." I slash one more time for effect and hear her giggle. "All clear," I say as I turn to her. She runs over to me, promptly pulls down her pants and briefs, and squats next to me as I do the same.

We finish up and make our way back to the car, Lilly doing a little skip as we go. She climbs in the back of the car and retrieves her teddy and then comes to stand by my side.

"I'm hungry," she whispers up to me.

"I know, Lilly. I'm working on it."

I open the trunk back up and pull out the bottle of water and take a long swallow before handing it over to her. She gulps it down greedily.

I want to tell her to slow down and to ration it, but then I see the can of pinto beans on the ground and decide to allow her this small satisfaction, since she's going to be eating her least favorite food today—and tomorrow... who knows what she'll be eating?

I start a small fire using dried sticks, which cut into the palms of my hands and make my blisters worse, but I'm getting good at making fires now; I'm much better at it than I used to be. Eventually the fire is burning well enough for me to heat the beans for her, and soon enough she's tucking into them with enough gusto to make me laugh.

"I thought you hated them," I say between drags of my cigarette.

"I do." She smiles and fills her cheeks, chewing greedily. "But I'm hungry."

My stomach grumbles loudly, and heat rises in my cheeks. I'm glad that I'm sitting down as a dizzy spell passes through me, making my empty stomach twist in on itself. The headache that has been building all morning eventually breaks free, and I feel momentarily blinded by the pulsing pain.

I squeeze my eyes closed, letting my cigarette burn down between my fingers until it singes the tips and I drop it with a yelp. When I open my eyes back up, Lilly is staring at me sadly, fork poised before her open mouth.

"You should eat," she whispers.

"I'm okay, I ate earlier," I lie.

Satisfied, she continues to eat, and I stand and sift through the first-aid kit until I find the last painkiller. I pop it in my mouth and grab the water bottle before realizing it is empty. I drop it back into the trunk of my car and pinch the bridge of my nose. Frustration and anger burn through me. Tears build behind my lids, but I force them back down as I dry swallow the powdery tablet, feeling it wedge in my throat. I continue to swallow until it starts to dissolve, leaving a vile, bitter taste in my mouth. At least it's down, is all I can think.

I turn to Lilly as she finishes the beans and lets out a small burp.

"All better now?"

She nods and smiles before picking up a stick and drawing in the dirt on the ground. Everything is dirty these days. Dirty and ruined.

Two.

It's early afternoon before the headache subsides enough for me to think clearly, and I approach Lilly with thoughts of a scavenger trip. As usual she instantly say no, but I press the matter with her. We have no water and no food. If we don't go today, we'll need to go tomorrow. We have no other choices. She doesn't reply, instead climbs into her chair without further words.

I pack our things back into the beat-up car and as I back out of our parking space, I pray that we have a safe trip and make it back up here before nightfall. I glance at Lilly in my rearview mirror. She's sulking, her hands wrapped tightly around her teddy, and her bottom lip poking out in a pout. She refuses to look at me, but she'll be happier when we have food and water. Perhaps I can find her a coloring book, or maybe a toy—anything would do at this point, though I know I'm grasping at straws.

My stomach gurgles in pain and anxiety as we drive away from our hilltop encampment. I climb out and pull the large gate back across, snapping the lock in place, and continue down the ruined road, dodging burnt out cars and dried out bones.

Our car leaves tracks in the dusty road, showing just how long we've been up here, and I'm satisfied that no one found this path—no monsters, no humans, no one. We are still safe, for now.

It's an hour or so before we are back in any form of civilization, if you can call it that now. Everything here has been picked clean—I should know, I've tried almost every house in the little sea-front town. I know that I'm going to have to go further afield this time, and that's even more worrying. At least here, I know more or less what to expect. I know where the nests of these things are, and I know most of the places to avoid. I roll down my window, letting the sea air into the car to help clear my thoughts. Stress eats away at my empty gut but I ignore the pain as best I can and grasp at memories of playing by the sea, the water washing between my toes.

I drive out of town with a worried sigh, and Lilly's voice whispers to me from the back seat.

"Where are we going?"

"There's nothing here anymore, nothing we can eat. We need to drive to a different town, one that will have food." I watch her in my mirror. Again, she doesn't argue with me on the matter, but looks away with another pout and begins to cry softly into her teddy bear. I think I'd prefer her to argue with me than cry. I wish there were another way, but there's not. Food is our goal. And of course a coloring book. She'll be happy then, I reason as I continue to drive, trying to ignore her soft whimpers.

After another hour or so of driving, passing nothing but ruined houses, buildings, and abandoned cars, I see a small turn-off on the left. I stop the car, get out, and examine the road, seeing no tracks of any sort—no telltale wheel marks or footprints, and even more thankfully, no claw marks from the monsters.

Satisfied, I take the turn and follow the ruined road upward between the trees, panicking when they become so tightly packed that they momentarily block out the daylight. Lilly has fallen asleep, and for that I'm glad. I don't think she would be happy about our current situation at all, and I'm not sure my gut could take any more guilt.

The road eventually opens up onto a long driveway, and right at the end is a circular island with a small fountain in the middle. Behind that is a huge mansion with enough windows to put a glass company to shame.

"Jesus," I murmur to myself. My stomach does a little flip, but my heart is excited. *This could be the mother lode*, I can't help but think as I send dust billowing up behind us.

I drive the car around the circular island in front of the house, pulling to a stop outside the large wooden front door. Lilly is still sleeping soundly, and I wonder whether to wake her or leave her be, thinking that the rest might do her good.

I step out and look to the sky. The sun is still high—there's plenty of daylight left—and we haven't seen anyone in months. I think she'll be okay here. It's probably safer in the sun than inside the danger of the shadows from the house.

I make my way to the front steps and peer in through a bottom window beside the wooden door. Nothing moves inside. The place is covered in a thin layer of dust, and again my heart flips in excitement. The front foyer of the house is like a greenhouse—more expensive glass lets in sunlight from every angle.

I walk around the perimeter of the house, checking in as many windows as I can, and find the same thing: dust-covered furniture and nothing more. Around the back of the house is a large barn area, and my head tells me that it's a prime monster hideout. I clench my knife tighter and head over to it as quietly as I can, stepping through the overgrown lawn and dried up flowerbeds.

I peer up at the barn, seeing gaps in the slats of wood where the sun can seep in, and I release the breath I've been holding as I brush my filthy hair away from my sweaty forehead. My hand tentatively touches the latch on the door. It's rusty and stiff, and will take both hands to push it up, meaning that I have to slip my knife into a back pocket so that I have the use of both hands—something I don't want to do, not even for a minute. If something is inside there, I need both hands free to fight. Indecision twists my gut, and with a heavy heart I put my knife away.

With shaking hands, I pull the door open wide, putting all my strength behind it. Sure, I could leave whatever might be in here to its own devices, but really, when night falls, if we're still here, the monsters will hunt us down and slaughter us like pigs. I have to check everywhere—for Lilly's sake as well as my own.

Sunlight explodes into the dark barn as I yank open the heavy door, and I wait for the sound of hissing and screaming, for the burning and toasting of graying flesh, but nothing happens. Dust motes floating in the thick, stagnant air are the only signs of movement within. A bubble of laughter tickles the back of my throat as my heart races wildly in my chest, rocketing a hundred miles an hour. I look inside the barn, safe from my place in the sun at the open doorway, seeing nothing of use: rusted old tools, horse saddles, engine parts. I shut the door, latch it too, and continue my perimeter search with a more confident step.

Arriving back at the front of the house, the trace of a smile graces my lips. From every window I looked through, the place seemed untouched by anything human or monster. No one and nothing has resided here for a long time. This means a couple of things: food could still be inside, and perhaps even a place to rest for the night. I squeeze away tears, which threaten to fall. Perhaps this place could be safe for a while.

My eyes fall on our car and fear ignites like a spark from a match: the back passenger door is wide open. I run to it and look inside. Both Lilly and her teddy bear are missing. I climb inside and check under the seats, scrambling out the other side of the car.

"Lilly?" I whisper shout. Panic ripens in my chest like a balloon being overfilled. I want to scream her name from the rooftops, but I can't.

I take a steadying breath and look around, trying to calm my raging emotions. I look at the ground, seeing little footprints at the side of the car. Without a doubt, they are her footprints. They head towards the house, and without a second thought, that's where I head too. I need to find my little Honey-Bee. My Lilly.

Three.

I follow her tiny footprints, trailing them towards the back of the house. My eyes flit to the barn, seeing the heavy door still closed like I left it. Her footsteps get lost in the overgrown grass, and I blink back furious tears—furious at myself for ever leaving her. She must have been so frightened when she woke, seeing that I wasn't there, and went looking for me.

I choke on a sob as I hear her voice calling my name, and I run—my leg muscles pumping, pushing foot ahead of foot in my eagerness to get to her.

I see her small frame by the back door, her little golden curls glistening in the sunshine as if spun from gold. She turns and sees me and begins to sob quietly as she hugs her teddy.

I reach her in seconds, my arms wrapping around her in a blanket of warm protectiveness, and I crush her small frame to me and kiss her head over and over as I blink back tears.

"I'm sorry, I'm so sorry, Lilly," I whisper into her hair.

Her body shakes in my arms.

"You left me," she whispers against my neck.

I shake my head. "No, never! I was just checking that everywhere was safe, and you were sleeping, and..." I hug her fiercely. "I'd never leave you. Never ever."

I pull out of the embrace to look into her face. Wetness covers her cheeks and I wipe it away with the back of my hand. She reaches out with her little porcelain fingers and wipes away mine. I kiss her fingertips.

"I'm sorry. I promise not to leave you again. Next time I'll wake you."

She nods, happy with my apology, though my heart is still beating furiously.

"Promise?"

"I promise. Cross my heart and hope to—" I don't finish the sentence.

"Can we go now?" she whispers.

"I think there may be food inside. I want to go in and look."

She shakes her head furiously. I know what she is thinking: the last time I went into a house, I nearly didn't make it out—but we need food and water and other basic things.

My stomach gurgles loudly and amusement flashes in her eyes. "See? Even my belly thinks it's safe to go inside." I laugh.

She takes a deep, shuddering breath and nods. I can tell that she is trying to be brave for me, and I'm grateful. I'm scared, too, so I can only imagine how she must feel. I balance her on my hip and go to the back door, looking through the closest window. I lean Lilly over so she can see too.

"See? The dust is settled, nothing has been in here for a long time," I say, looking into her large brown eyes, trying to offer her some reassurance.

She peers in again and then looks back at me. "No monsters?"

"I don't think so," I reply.

"No people?"

My heart pains for her. "I don't think so. We have to try, Lilly."

She juts out her bottom lip, but nods all the same.

"I need to put you down for a minute. I need to break the lock." She shakes her head, her fingers digging into me. "I have to." I gently pry her white-knuckled grip away from me; her chin quavers, but she relents and slowly slides to the ground.

I dig the tip of my knife into the keyhole and jiggle it around, hoping that it will magically unlock, but nothing happens. I look through the window again and huff until I feel Lilly tug on my jeans leg and I look down to her.

She points to the small cat flap at the bottom of the door. "I can't fit through there, honey." She continues to stare at me, eyes wide, frightened, and glossy as she points again. I look from the flap to her and get her meaning.

"I want to help." She whispers so quietly I barely hear her.

I shake my head. "No, no way. Anything could be in there."

Her brow scrunches up. "You said that there were no monsters."

"I don't think there are."

"You said there were no people."

I rub my forehead, my headache coming back with a vengeance. "I said I don't think there is anyone in there. I can't say for certain on anything." Dizziness overcomes me and I know I need to sit down. The heat beating down on me, the worry, and the lack of food in my system have all built up to such a level that I feel faint again. I sit, lowering my head between my knees, and take a deep breath.

What I'd do for a drink of water now. I close my eyes, feeling Lilly's little hand on my shoulder, patting me in an attempt to comfort. Her head rests a second later near the same spot. She knows that I'm getting sick; I was a fool to think I could hide it from her.

I keep my eyes closed as I concentrate on my breathing, listening to the steady thrum of my heartbeat and the birds chirping in the sky. Time stands still, or perhaps it waits for me to catch up.

I know something is wrong when my head feels heavy and it drops suddenly between my knees as I nod off and wake myself up all in the same fraction of a second.

I jump and grab for my knife as my eyes spring open. I stand quickly when I find Lilly to be missing again.

"Lilly?" I spin on the spot looking for her, my eyes landing on the cat flap as I step up to the window and look inside. She's on the other side of the door, reaching up from her tiptoes to snag the lock open, but she's too small. Her wide eyes see me at the window and she gives a little shrug. I look past her into the room behind, hoping to find something she can stand on, but see nothing but coats and shoes.

I crouch down to the ground and push the cat flap up as I peer inside. Lilly's face comes nose to nose with me a moment later, her cheeks flushed.

"I can't reach."

"I know, Lilly. Don't worry. Come out now."

"I could go look for a chair."

"No. I want you to come out." Pain flashes behind my eyes, rocking my body and making me gasp. "Come out right now," I say between clenched teeth. I sit back on my haunches to catch my breath as hunger pangs run tight across my abdomen. I pull out my cigarettes with shaking hands and light one immediately in the hopes that it will again take away the hunger pangs, which are becoming more and more frequent. I watch the little door for Lilly, frowning when she doesn't come straight out, and poke the door upwards with my hand while exhaling smoke out of the side of my mouth. "Lilly?" I see her little feet tiptoeing away. "Get back out here now!" I whisper urgently.

She looks back over her shoulder but ignores my request and keeps going until she's out of view from my vantage point. I stand quickly, throw my cigarette away, and stare through the glass. I curse in hushed whispers when I still can't see her and run to the next one along to try and find her. Nothing but a heavy leather armchair and some crowded bookcases fill this room—no Lilly, no monsters, and no danger. I move to the next window, seeing the back of her pass by the room and on to the next one.

I quickly move along the building to the next window, watching as she peeks around the doorway, her curls catching the sunlight shining through the window. She looks out at me with a shy smile. I smile back and point to the corner where a small wooden chair rests, covered with yellow, aging paperwork. Lilly totters over, pulls everything off it, and attempts to pick up the chair. It's only a small chair, but she's so little herself and can't wrap her arms around it. She looks to me, then back to the chair, stubbornness etched across her sweet features as she clasps its wooden back in her fingers and begins to drag it behind her.

She drags the chair out of the room and down the long hallway. I cringe at the sound of the wood scraping along the wooden floor, feeling helpless standing outside. I look behind me and then up, seeing that the clouds have begun to gather for a storm, effectively blocking out the sun's protective rays.

Panic burns my chest. We need to get going soon or we won't make it back in time. I look back in the window, the shadow of something passing the doorway a split second later. It's so quick I'm unsure if I actually saw it or if it was just my imagination. Seconds later, Lilly's piercing scream cuts the air, realizing my nightmare, and I feel my heart freeze in my chest.

Four.

I spring back up the side of the building to the stupid little cat flap, peering through it on hands and knees.

Lilly is holding the chair in front of her, its legs pointing at the monster hissing at her. It stays back, away from the light shining in from the window, keeping to the shadows of the doorway.

"Lilly!" I yell. "Open the door, Lilly!"

The monster looks at me, its eyes glowing a deeper red as it bares its mouthful of sharp teeth at me. Its nails click-clack against the wooden floor as it steps forward, but the sun touches its skin and sends it squealing like a pig and scooting back into the shadows again.

Lilly continues to cower behind the chair, her body racked with sobs.

"Open the door, Lilly. Use the chair," I plead.

She never takes her eyes from the monster, her fingers clasped tightly to the wooden slats of the chair as her body shakes and fat tears fall freely down her cherub cheeks.

I clamber to my feet and look to the sky, clouds overhead continuing to build. Please, no. The sunlight is our only protection. I look in through the window again. The monster continues to stare at Lilly. Only once do its eyes stray to me, almost as if it can sense that she is the meal and there is nothing I can do about it. I bang my fist on the glass in frustration, making Lilly jump and the thing hiss. I look back to the sky again; clouds continue to fill it. Panic fills me to the brim, threatening to explode from my chest at any moment.

"Damn it." I pull down the sleeve on my sweater covering the end of my hand as I slam it against the glass. After my first attempt doesn't break the glass, I hit it again until it finally smashes through, sending splinters raining down to the floor.

I climb up and through the hole, catching myself on several shards of glass and feeling my blood ooze from me, all the while my knife gripped tightly in the palm of my hand. I fall to the floor clumsily, scooting backwards and putting myself between Lilly and the monster.

"You're okay now. I'm here," I whisper through ragged breaths. She continues to sob quietly behind me. "I'll protect you, I'll always protect you," I say with more conviction than I truly believe.

A shadow falls across the room and the monster sidles closer, a look of almost glee on its distorted face. I want to sob and cry and stamp my foot at the unfairness of it all. There's food here, I know there is. We're so close.

The shadows deepen, making the thing almost at touching distance. It stalks backwards and forward, watching us, waiting, biding its time. Its fingers and toes curl and uncurl, teeth constantly bared and hungry as it snaps at the air. I glance to the window, seeing the last of the sun finally covered by darkened clouds heavy with rainfall, as the monster pounces with a sound almost like a cackle. My knife quickly comes up from my side, catching it off guard, and slashes it deeply in the stomach. I twist and pull, feeling leathery flesh tearing. It continues to snap at me, screeching in my face, its teeth snapping to find purchase even as its eyes widen in pain.

I hold it back, one hand gripping tightly to its throat, and plunge my knife deeper into its gut with my other. It can't have my Lilly. I hear the telltale slop of insides tumbling to the floor and kick out at it. It falls backwards, its legs and arms stilling.

My breath is ragged in my throat, and Lilly is still crying, almost wailing uncontrollably behind me. I turn and scoop her up into my arms and squeeze her trembling body close to me as we both gasp for air. This isn't the first of these that I've killed, but it was the easiest kill, and considering that I'm so undernourished and weak, I struggle to work out how that is possible. Is it conceivable that they could be weakening too? That after gorging on the human race and purging us to near extinction, they are now slowly starving? The thought both saddens me and makes me rejoice—to think that they could be weakening, dying even.

I climb over its destroyed body with Lilly clinging to my side, her face buried in my neck. I step into the dim hallway, fear driving me forward when I should probably be running to my car—but for what? For how long?

Sooner or later I'll be too weak to protect her, too weak to get her anywhere safe, and then my little Lilly will be all alone in the world with no one to look after her. Better I find us food now and stay alive for a little longer.

The house is huge—huge and quiet. Dark shadows play against every wall, steps echoing around us. The thunder starts outside, the pitter-patter of heavy raindrops against the windows of the many rooms. Lilly stops crying; only the occasional snivel comes from her still form against my hip. She's getting heavy, or I'm getting more tired. The adrenaline is wearing off, but fear is still running rampant. The two things collide in my head, making me feel dizzy and unsteady on my feet. I sway into the wall, feeling Lilly stiffen.

"I'm okay, Honey-Bee, I'm okay." I kiss the top of her head and push off from the wall with blurring vision, terror filling me. I'm so close. I continue to walk until the narrow hallway opens up to an entrance hall. A large glass window in the circular ceiling makes the space bright and welcoming—more so than the rest of the house, anyway. Lightning flashes, causing our shadows to move and make me jump. Lilly begins to sob again. I can feel her warm tears trickling down my neck.

I head to the front door and look out the windows, seeing our car there, seeing freedom, but again, I know I can't leave here without food. Hell, we probably can't leave here at all tonight. Not with this storm. The streets will more than likely be swarming with the monsters.

I move away from the window and head down a different hallway, finding room after empty room. The house is covered in a thick layer of dust and I can't fathom where the hell the thing had been hiding, or if there are any more. No footsteps mark their presence, no claw marks or piles of bones. Nothing. I want to ask Lilly if she saw where it had come from, but don't want to frighten her any more than she already is. I somehow, mercifully, stumble upon the kitchen, my heart jittering in my chest as I make my way to one of the large cupboards and look inside. Disappointment rings in my ears at the sight of plates and bowls. I try the next one and find something similar. A sob clogs my airway as I open a third cupboard, and my eyes bulge as I finally see can after can of food, and I sob loudly.

"Lilly," I whisper. She doesn't move and I whisper her name again until she pulls her face free of me; I twist her on my hip so she can see the food and I let out a small laugh of glee. We made it.

She blinks away her tears and stares in awe at the food before finally turning to me with a wide smile. She lifts a pointing finger to the food and I nod and step closer for her. She plucks a can free from the shelf with her chubby hands: fruit. She smiles again and bounces on my hip, and I quietly laugh again.

We're going to be okay. For now, we're going to be okay.

Five.

A new morning has come and gone and early afternoon welcomed us with a sunny smile—yesterday's storm has disappeared like a bad dream. We wake almost simultaneously, the glare from the sun a happy sight upon our faces. Lilly hugs me closer and I squeeze an arm around her little body, feeling bones jutting out. But it's okay now—there's food here, lots of it. We ate like pigs last night, and today we'll do the same. And the day after too. We'll fill our stomachs, put meat on our bones, and live for a little longer. I sigh contentedly.

We root through the dusty, overfilled closets and find clean clothes, piling our old tatty ones into a heap in the corner. I roll the sleeves up for Lilly, and do the same with the pants.

It makes me sad, when we find a child's bedroom, to think that once there had been someone only a little older than my Lilly living here. I can't help but wonder what happened to them. Did they make it out alive? I hope so. God, I hope so.

When the world went to hell, the planet rocked, reeling from the realization that such evil could live among us in plain sight. We were nearly destroyed, but as confusion and fear gave way to anger, we came back. When the second wave attacked, we were prepared and we fought. God, how we fought. But for every monster killed, two would replace it, until the human race fled and hid.

It has been one year, six months, three weeks, and nineteen days, and Lilly and I have only ever stumbled across a handful of living people. They were not good people. They were desperate and afraid, and with that desperation and fear came violence. There is now more to fear in this world than the monsters. Man is now its own enemy.

I shake my head free of those thoughts. I don't want to think about those people now. We're here, and I have everything I need for now: Lilly, clean clothes, food, and water—I even found some more smokes. This place won't be safe forever, but it is for now. For today at least, and in this world, you live day to day.

My head feels a little better today, but the low throb of starvation still burns in my gut and make my brain ache, so I take two painkillers from the medicine cabinet we found and swallow them down with flat pop from the larder in the kitchen. Flat pop never tasted so good, I muse.

Lilly sits happily at the kitchen counter, a bowl of dried cereal on one side of her and a coloring book in front. Some of the pictures are already colored in, and it makes me sad, but Lilly says that it makes her happy, that a piece of the child that lived here still goes on in this world. That makes me happier.

Lilly feels safe here, in a house with walls and beds and toys to play with. I can't deny that the feeling of carpet between my toes isn't something to appreciate.

I finish my breakfast and leave Lilly in the sunny entrance hall; it seems the safest place for her, given all the windows and the glare coming in from the sun. I've checked every inch of this house and found nothing and no one else here. A small, downstairs, windowless bathroom is where I find the blood and bones of whoever once lived here—the place where the monster had been sleeping.

Like it had gone into some sort of stasis after a while, trapped between the sunlight from one room and the shade of the bathroom with no windows. Hope blossoms in my heart that maybe the world could come back from this. There must be people somewhere working on a cure, a way to kill them off, or turn them back to what they used to be.

I step up to the back door, unlatch it, and swing it open wide, letting in sunlight and fresh air. I reach down for the monster's ankles and begin to drag it outside, wondering why it doesn't burn up when the sunlight touches it now that it's dead. Its head bumps harshly against the doorframe and leaves a dark black stain.

I continue to drag it out onto the lawn, away from the house, before grabbing some of the old newspapers I have brought with me and laying them across the body of the man. I tuck some inside the jacket of his suit, up his sleeves and up his pants legs.

I guess this was the father—before he became the monster. I shake my head sadly and stand back up, pulling the matches from my pocket. I strike one, and with hesitance, I throw it on the body.

I watch him burn, his skin crackling and popping, melting back from his face, lips stretching back to reveal the tiny pointed teeth caked in black. As his hair fizzes and pops, the smell reminds me to step back, the scent getting too strong. I look towards the back door, seeing Lilly standing there watching. I gesture for her to come over and she does, and I pick her up automatically.

We watch as the monster burns, revealing a more primitive form: that of a man. The man he once was, before all of this happened. It kills me to think that he was like me once, yet somehow he turned into this thing, this monster. From the bones I found, he killed his own family. The raw animalistic instinct taking over him must have been agonizing, and I have to believe that he fought against it with everything he had.

"Will I become like that one day?" Lilly asks quietly.

"Not if I can help it," I reply without hesitation.

"But that's what happens, isn't it?"

I don't reply, but look her in the eye with a soft smile. "You'll never be one of them. I promise you." Of course, I can't promise her. There are no promises in this world anymore.

"I don't want to be a monster." She hugs me.

"I know. And I won't let you. We have food and water, and we'll be okay for a little while now." I rub the hair back from her face, seeing the dark trail of poisoned black blood in her veins reaching up like paths on a map. I know I have them too. Everyone does. "You'll always be my Honey-Bee. Okay?"

She nods. "Okay." She looks towards the burning corpse and then back to me. "Can we go color some more?"

I smile. "Of course."

We walk back toward the house, and I swallow down the tears that threaten to flow. How long do we have left? A week? A month? A year? I have no idea. But at least we have food and water now. For now, there is hope of a cure, and the promise of life.

We'll be okay for now, me and my Honey-Bee.

About Claire C. Riley

Claire C Riley is a #1 Best Selling British Horror writer. Her work is best described as the modernization of classic, old-school horror. She fuses multi-genre elements to develop storylines that pay homage to cult-classics while still feeling fresh and cutting-edge. She writes characters that are realistic, and kills them without mercy.

Claire lives in the UK with her husband, three daughters, and one scruffy dog.

Her works namely include, old school vampires and apocalyptic zombie ridden worlds, with several full-length books, and short stories to her name, with plenty more coming up in 2014.

Awards and Accreditations

Odium. The Dead Saga is a top #100 dystopian selling book on Amazon.com for 2013, 'Indie book of the day' winner December 2013 and 'Indie Author Land 50 best self-published books worth reading 2013/14'

Limerence featured book in the 'Guardian newspaper for best Indie novel 2013' and is currently a finalist for the eFestival of Words 'best novel' category.

Odium II The Dead Saga is a #1 Best Selling British Horror book.

She is also a very proud contributor to the 'Let's Scare Cancer to Death' charity anthology.

She can be stalked at any of the following.

www.clairecriley.com
https://www.facebook.com/ClaireCRileyAuthor
http://bit.ly/clairecrileyamazon/
https://twitter.com/ClaireCRiley
https://www.google.com/+ClaireCRiley

Armand Rosamilia

Introduction to "Dying Days: Fear of the Dark", by Armand Rosamilia

I write some pretty over the top things in my extreme zombie series, Dying Days... the zombies don't want to just bite you, they want to sexually violate you. But this story isn't about those monsters, its about something far worse: your fellow man. I wanted to see how deep I could get into one character, and I came away having to take a shower and hug my kids afterwards. I hope you feel the same way.

Dying Days: Fear of the Dark

Water dripped from the rusting pipes overhead, just out of reach in the basement. Derek remembered seeing the orange stains, the rotting ceiling and the many chains curled down from the low rafters.

Weeks ago, when he'd been taken from the refugee camp, was the last time he'd seen his parents. The last time he'd seen the sun or tasted freedom, such as it was in this dying world.

He cried every time the overhead light was out because the darkness scared him. He'd had a Winnie the Pooh nightlight in his room that he was too old to still have but mother wouldn't let father take it away. But he knew it would've been sooner than later.

Even after graduating high school he kept the nightlight. Derek knew what a disappointment he was to his father. He was small for his age, he was weak, and he still looked like a teen. His father had no use for a son who couldn't catch a football or understand the difference between a fastball and a sinker.

He was strapped naked to the metal chair, his flesh hot during the day and cold at night. Derek was not allowed to eat or release his bladder unless Socks Man said.

Derek called him Socks Man because that is all he ever wore, a pair of dirty white knee-high socks. The thought of Socks Man coming down the wooden stairs frightened him, because there was always a price to pay when he did. Not once had he simply held Derek's privates and let him pee or fed him the cold Ramen noodles without then getting what he wanted.

It was so absolute blackness Derek couldn't see his body when he looked down. Was this Hell? Was he dead and didn't know it yet? He thought he was alive because he could feel the blisters on his back and ass when he moved even slightly.

He didn't know what day it was but knew he'd slept at least a dozen times since someone had put a sack over his head before hitting him in the temple.

He wanted to see his parents again. And tell them that he loved them.

*

"Wake if you want to eat," Socks Man said loudly.

Derek opened his eyes and looked away at the nakedness before him.

Socks Man laughed. "You don't find me attractive? How do you know? You're too young to properly judge. Have you had other men?"

Derek closed his eyes. He was very hungry but knew as soon as he was done eating Socks Man would do something disgusting to him. Often, Derek threw up afterwards. He put his head down and opened his eyes to see the stains where the food had fallen on previous days.

"Do you need to pee?"

Derek nodded.

"Do you need to poop?"

Derek nodded again.

"Why don't you ever talk?" Socks Man asked.

Derek looked up into the man's bloodshot eyes. "I... didn't know I was allowed."

Socks Man smiled but it wasn't pleasant. "You are very obedient. I like that, Derek."

"How do you know my name?"

Socks Man put the bowl of food on the card table next to him and clapped. The thin yellow light from the overhead bulb cast grotesque shadows on the four walls, not penetrating the shadows. "It speaks."

"My name is Derek."

Socks Man frowned. "Your name is It. You are worthless. Like a piece of garbage. No one loves you except for me. Your parents gave you away."

"That isn't true. You took me," Derek said. At the thought of his parents he began to cry.

"Suck it up, Cupcake. Your parents are long gone. They either escaped to die another day or when the zombies overran the camp they were ripped apart." Socks Man looked at the ceiling. "Maybe they're upstairs, even now, waiting to come down and eat you. And do bad things to you." Socks Man looked at Derek. "I do bad things to you, but it's only because I can now."

"You won't get away with this," Derek said defensively, knowing how stupid he sounded. "My father will kill you."

"Your father left you. He ran like a bitch when the fences came down. He didn't grab you like in a cheesy movie and rush you to safety. Your mother didn't cover you and protect you. They ran for their lives and left you for dead. I saved you. You should be thankful instead of being such a crybaby."

"I want to go home," Derek said quietly.

Socks Man smiled. "Where is home?"

Derek hesitated before finally answering. "Baltimore."

Socks Man laughed. "You're a long way from Baltimore, It. Do you even know where you are?"

"We were in Delaware, I think." It had all been a blur over the weeks before his capture. His mother had woken Derek in the middle of the night and telling him to pack a suitcase. Father, looking like he'd been crying and looking scared, throwing everything he could fit into the trunk and backseat of their car. No one talking as they drove. His father made a comment to his wife about having a son who still didn't have a driver's license to help with the burden. Derek remembered the main highways were blocked with abandoned cars and people running across the median and into the nearby streets or into the woods.

There had been an explosion up ahead and Mother held him to her chest as Derek cried while father got mad. He remembered walking down a trail in the woods with hundreds of other people, all dragging suitcases and even two men lugging a flat-screen television.

Derek remembered the camp with the chain-link fences, the one the military men with rifles told them they'd be safe in. The camp everyone was piled on top of one another and it stunk like urine and smelly bodies.

"Yes, you were in Delaware. So was I. But I went because I wanted to, not because I was shuffled like cattle or sheep to the slaughter. I went to Delaware because of you." Socks Man grinned. "I knew you were the one as soon as I saw you."

"What do you mean?"

"Do you think you're the only special one I ever found and took back to my basement? I've been doing this for years, and I've never been caught. I've never even been a suspect. You know why? Because I'm smart. I fly under the radar. I pay my taxes, I mow my lawn and I go bowling on Tuesday night and wave at the neighbors. I drive the speed limit. I don't eat weird foods or draw attention to myself. I do what I need to do to blend in with society. It is the best place to be when you want to steal a little piece of normal society for yourself."

Derek was very hungry and had to go to the bathroom but he also wanted Socks Man to stay and keep the light on. He hated the dark. He was scared of being alone, and whenever he heard a noise he'd cry again. Mother used to say the house was settling but he feared the monsters under his bed and in the closet. His father would scream for him to grow up and act his age.

Socks Man was the thing he needed to fear more than the dark, though. "How many?"

"How many what?"

"You said I wasn't the first," Derek said. He didn't know if he really wanted to hear the answer and knew he was stalling. Now that he was allowed to talk without getting beaten, he decided to see how long it would last. "How many other men and women have sat in this chair?"

"Quite a few." Socks Man crossed his arms. He was old. Older than maybe even Derek's parents, and his flesh was white and doughy. He was covered in hair like an ape, and his man parts were hidden in all the coarse hair.

"I've been doing it on and off for years. Without being caught. Now there is no one to catch me. As long as I stay away from important people and children no one raises much of a stink. Some eighteen year old stoner or a twenty-something unemployed slacker doesn't get the news and local police too worried. People like that drift off to California or Florida with their buddies all the time."

"Someone will stop you," Derek said.

"Who?"

Derek had no answer.

Socks Man picked up the bowl of food. "Are you hungry?"

"I have to pee."

Socks Man smiled. "You have many things to do."

*

"What is your name?" Derek asked a few hours or a few days later. He'd lost count and had no sensible way to keep track. It was all a blur and he spent more and more time weak and sleeping in a sitting position.

"Why do you care?"

"I care. My name is Derek."

Socks Man dropped the plate and smacked Derek across the face, splitting his lip.

"Your name is It. Don't you ever talk back to me again. This is why I wish I had cigarettes and a match, because I'd burn your tongue from your mouth," Socks man said. He scooped up some of the oatmeal from the dirty floor and shoved it into Derek's mouth. "Eat or this will be your last meal."

Derek closed his eyes and chewed.

*

His mother had slapped him once for talking back at the dinner table when his father had been away for business. Derek must've been about seven and he asked his mother why daddy had left them. It had struck a nerve because she'd reached across the table in one swift move and struck him, knocking him off of his chair and to the floor.

Derek still remembered how straight his mother's legs were under the table. He lay stunned until she'd finally told him to stop being so dramatic and asking questions and finish his dinner.

They'd never spoken of it, and a week later Father returned and his parents spent a full day in their room, crying and arguing before finally emerging with smiles.

It was the only time he'd ever been struck in his life before he'd met Socks Man.

*

"I have a treat for you, It. I found some meat." Socks Man had a small plate in his hands and was smiling. "It's all for you."

"Why are you being nice?" Derek didn't trust the man. He'd never been nice before. Not even close. "Is it poisoned?"

"Why would I poison the meat when I have you bound to a chair? How stupid would that be? If I wanted to kill you I could do it ninety-nine ways. All of them cooler than poisoning." Socks Man turned away, showing Derek his pale white ass. "I guess I'll eat it myself. And you can skip a meal."

"Wait..."

Sock Man turned around slowly and grinned. "Yes?"

"I want to eat."

"Eat what?"

"The food."

Socks Man held up the plate. "What food? What is it?"

"The meat," Derek said and sighed. He knew where this was going from previous conversations. This wasn't going to be pleasant.

"Who's meat?"

Derek looked at the plate of meat.

"Who's meat?" Socks Man repeated.

"Your meat."

Socks Man laughed. "Haha, I like when I get you to say stuff without having to punch you in the face first." He went up to Derek. "Open your mouth so I can feed you."

When Derek was sure it wasn't a trick, and ignoring the man's nakedness, he opened wide.

Socks Man shoved a fistful of food into Derek's mouth and nearly choked him.

Derek began chewing, swallowing the meat with delight. It tasted odd and he wasn't sure he'd ever had it before, but it wasn't that bad. Especially when most of the food he'd been fed were noodles, soup and crackers no matter what meal it was.

"You want another bite?" Socks Man asked, dangling the food in his fingers. "It wants another taste?"

Derek nodded, licking his lips so he got every last morsel.

Socks Man smelled the meat and grimaced, shaking his head. "You little idiot. Do you know what I'm feeding you? Dog food. I found a can of dog food at the neighbor's house next door. That bitch had four or five dogs.

I hate pets. They're stupid and they make a mess. I wish the back door hadn't been broken into because I would've gone in and caught the dogs and grilled them in the backyard. You would've eaten dog and cat meat for dinner tonight. How does that sound?"

"Um... not good," Derek said, but his stomach grumbled. The thought of meat cooking on the grill like Father used to do made his mouth water. Mother would shuck corn and they'd wrap it and put them on the grill with fresh vegetables. Derek could smell it now and he missed lazy summer days, swimming in the pool with his few friends until the neighbors would come over and there'd be a nightly cookout.

"I'm going to find a dog or hamster and grill it and make you eat it. Then I'll really laugh," Socks Man said. He turned to walk away.

"Where are you going?" Derek asked.

Socks Man looked down at the plate and then at Derek and smiled. "I was going to throw this shit out. It's dog food. Not fit for human consumption, It. Even though I don't think you're necessarily human, I don't want you eating this garbage. You know how much filler is in this? All kinds of crazy steroids and pieces of shoe leather and whatnot. You could contract anthrax from it."

"I'm hungry," Derek said quietly.

Socks Man stared at the plate silently for a few minutes while Derek watched.

"Fine. I don't care. More Ramen noodle for me," Socks Man said. "Too bad for you I only found one can. I could feed you for weeks on a bag of dry food."

*

Derek woke in the dark and his fear didn't subside. He shut his eyes, replacing one dark for another. At least with his eyes shut he could pretend he was safe.

Father always said he was going to get over his fear of the dark and stop using the nightlight and grow up like everyone else, but Derek knew right here and right now he'd never get over it.

Something banged loudly overhead. Had a noise woken him? He had no idea what time it was or how long he'd been sleeping. His arms were numb and even breathing hurt the sores on his back, butt and legs.

Another loud noise, this time sounding like something metal dropping to the floor. Derek had a general sense right above him was probably the kitchen, since he could sometimes hear Socks Man running water and the overhead pipes dripping more.

Now he could hear the muffled yells of Socks Man. Who else was up there with him? Could it be Father, come to rescue Derek?

Derek began struggling with his restraints but he was too weak and they were still too tight. If he could manage to slip out of his bonds...

He was about to yell for his father when he heard two gunshots, followed by three more in rapid succession. There were several people upstairs and he heard Socks Man shouting and things breaking. Something fragile fell to the kitchen floor and shattered.

The basement door opened and the light came on, which was a relief for Derek.

Until he saw Socks Man take a step down, slam the door behind him, and stumble down the stairs. His left arm was a bloody mess, and Derek could see bone sticking out. His left shoulder was also bleeding.

"What happened? Is my father here?"

Socks Man snorted. He was breathing heavily. "No... damn biters broke into my house... I got bit."

Something heavy slammed into the door above.

Derek struggled against the restraints. "Let me go."

"Why would I do that?"

"Because you're going to turn into one of them. You're going to bite me," Derek said. He started to panic. "Please... let me live. I need to find my parents."

Socks Man stumbled over and sat on the other chair in the room, slumping and staring at Derek. "I'm not going to let you go. It was never an option."

"Things have changed. You won't live longer than an hour or two, and you know it. Give me a chance to get away."

Socks Man groaned softly, blood dripping between his fingers as he tried to cover the gaping wound in his shoulder.

"I want to live," Derek said quietly.

"I want chocolate ice cream. Neither of us is going to get what we want today, buddy. Just shut up and relax. Your life was over the second I saw you in the camp. The second your mommy turned away to see where your daddy was leading you. It was too easy. In all the chaos I took what I wanted."

"Let me go," Derek pleaded. He was crying and he began to shake.

"You'll be my last. You might even be my favorite. You've definitely lasted longer than any of the others, It. And you obeyed and serviced me well. I'll miss you," Socks Man said.

"Let me go. I won't tell anyone."

"There's no one to tell. Everyone is dead but you and I. And guess what, It? I'll be joining the ranks of the biters very soon." Socks Man smiled. "The best part is the fact I still get you all to myself."

"My name is Derek."

Socks Man smiled. "Do you want to hear something ironic, It? Do you know what irony is?"

Derek shook his head. He could see Socks Man changing by the second, the bites festering and his skin running with black veins and puss replacing some of the blood leakage.

"My name is also Derek." He stood and stared at the boy. "I'm about to die."

"Then release me... please."

"I can't. I just can't." He began to shake, his arm trembling as the blood slowed to a trickle. "I can offer you one option and one only."

"What?" Derek asked, giving up on getting off of the metal chair.

"I'm going to turn into a zombie in a few seconds and then I'm going to bite you and snuff the life from you. Which is my right, you know. Do you want to see it coming, or should I turn off the light?"

Derek closed his eyes and sat up in the chair. "Do it in the dark."

About Armand Rosamilia

Armand Rosamilia is a New Jersey boy currently living in sunny Florida, where he writes when he's not watching the Boston Red Sox and listening to Heavy Metal music...

He's written over 100 stories that are currently available, including a few different series

"Dying Days" extreme zombie series

"Keyport Cthulhu" horror series

"Flagler Beach Fiction Series" contemporary fiction

"Metal Queens" non-fiction music series

He also loves to talk in third person... because he's really that cool. He's a proud Active member of HWA as well.

You can find him at http://armandrosamilia.com for not only his latest releases but interviews and guest posts with other authors he likes!

E-mail him to talk about zombies, baseball and Metal: armandrosamilia@gmail.com

Jack Wallen

Introduction to "My Own Terms", by Jack Wallen

"My Own Terms" came about because I first wrote the wrong story. Or, I should say, I wrote the right story in the wrong voice. My plan was to create an environment or situation that clearly displayed a global hopelessness, but two things happened – first and foremost, I was attempting to write hard sci-fi (not my thing). Second, and this is crucial, I wound up writing something that had no intimacy, no way for the reader to place themselves into a hopeless situation and understand exactly how desperate the human animal can be.

When an author finishes a story and says "Who cares?" about his or her own work, that's a powerful slam to the gut. The second those words were uttered, that first story was scrapped and My Own Terms came to be.

I wanted to write something claustrophobic, bleak, desperate... something that could drain the life out of the characters and the readers, something with just the right mixture of trope and scope that would make you, upon completing the story, shake your head and be happy it wasn't you.

Challenge accepted!

Challenge accomplished? That is up for you to decide. In the end, however, "My Own Terms" came out in my own voice and that, my friends, is what it's all about for an author – being honest to their own, unique, craft.

This story will wind up in the I Zombie series. I'm not sure how and I'm not sure when...but I cannot let this idea go to waste. I hope you agree. I hope you enjoy.

I also hope you cringe a bit.

My Own Terms

I was still breathing. At least there was that. Though it came in ragged gasps, I could judge my state of being by the need to pull in oxygen. Other than that...I wasn't so sure. My skin was cold and my vision tunneled. Out of habit, two fingers shot up to my neck to take a pulse.

Metal. The cold touch of metal prevented my fingers from reaching the beat of my carotid artery. Both hands reached up to grasp what felt like an over-sized metallic cuff around my neck.

Panic flooded my system. I knew I was alive. I had to be, but how?

And why?

And what in the world was happening?

"Hello?" I shouted.

My call was greeted by a low, menacing laugh. I glanced around, but the tunnel vision had me short sighted in more ways than I cared.

"Who's there? My name is David Schofield. I am the head of Thoracic Surgery at Brown-Pitman."

I tried to stand. My legs buckled.

It was then that I put a semblance of two and two together. I'd been drugged and kidnapped. But to what end? I tossed my mind backwards to attempt to catch a trace of memory that would lead me from some point A to this point B.

If only my vision would return in earnest.

Emotion begged I panic. Logic, fortunately, held powerful sway over that which could easily undo this situation. So, I did the one thing my therapist always insisted I practice. I sat and focused on the moment. What did I see, what did I hear, what did I smell? Those things which would never lie, never lead me astray.

I heard echoing cries and the squeal and clank of metallic doors.

I smelled piss and body odor.

I saw...vertical bars.

My legs were still unable to stand, so I crawled. My knees and hands carried me to the end of my journey -- when my head cracked into a row of metal bars. My hands shot out before me; knuckles cracked on unforgiving metal.

Again, the laughing sound.

"Who's there?"

I was met with silence.

"I asked, who's there?"

"Your cell mate." The voice was deep, raw, aggressive.

My hands released the bars and I flipped my body so my back was against the wall.

"Why have we been incarcerated?"

The laugh returned. "Damn, you use some big ass words. Oh, yeah...you're a doctor. I hate to tell you this, but inside here, we're all seen as equal."

The pulse I was so desperate to find earlier, made a sterling entrance. "What do you mean by 'all'?"

"Take a listen. What do you hear?"

I did. Understanding instantly flooded my system.

"What is this place?" I asked, my voice developed a desperate undertone.

"The end."

"I don't understand."

The stranger released a heavy sigh. I pinned my sight his way and watched his blurry form stand. "It's where they bring the living to study the dead."

"I don't understand."

"How in the fuck is it that someone using words like you doesn't understand shit? They dragged my ass off the street and I get it."

Panic pushed aside desperation for the moment.

"What is this thing around my neck?" My voice cracked. I could feel spit fly from between my lips.

"That's so they can control you. You'll do what they say when you finally learn what that thing is."

"Why don't you tell me?"

"Not my place."

Silence.

"Please."

"Sorry."

"You have to –"

"Mother fucker, I don't have to do shit," the stranger shouted.

The violent burst of anger sent me scooting back into a corner, where I remained.

No more words were spoken. I blinked against my blurry vision – to no avail. As my eyes opened and closed, my body became weary. All I could think about was sleep.

I closed my eyes until a myoclonic seizure jerked me back into the world of the waking.

"Sucks don't it?" The stranger intoned just above a whisper. "Locked up in a cage and you can't even get no sleep."

"Get any sleep," I corrected.

"What?"

"You used a double negative in that sentence. You said 'Can't even get no sleep'. Can't and no are negatives, so you effectively said I could get sleep."

"Crazy ass cock sucker. You're wanting to make this game easy on me, aren't you?"

My curiosity was instantly piqued. "Game? What do you mean by game?"

Silence.

"No, no, no. Tell me what you meant."

Silence.

"God damn it," I shouted. "Tell me what you meant by game!"

"Whoa, brotha, you'll learn soon enough. If I teach you what's what, they give me the juice. How's about you drag your skinny white ass up onto that bunk and get some rest. When they tell you...you'll know what the fuck's up. Until then...enjoy your ignorance."

Fear threatened to ignite my rage and have me shouting for justice. I had a feeling there was little to be found. I decided it was best to take the stranger's advice and do something I rarely did...relish in ignorance.

I also followed his first piece of advice and pulled myself up onto the nearby bunk. The second my head hit what could only roughly be called a pillow, my breathing grew shallow and I succumbed to the siren song of sleep.

*

The crash of metal jerked me back into the land of the living. My heart raced, my skin tingled with the flood of adrenaline.

"What's going on," I called out to the stranger.

"Time for your education, my friend. Sit up and prepare yourself for the new world order."

"Why? What's..."

Before I could finish my sentence, a cart was rolled in front of the cell.

"Hey," I shouted...and was succinctly ignored. "I want some answers, now. And I want to speak with my lawyer."

Laughter ignited from every direction.

"You crack my shit up, man." My cellmate's rumble of a voice silenced my cries.

My vision had finally returned, so I could take in the behemoth that was the man who shared my cell. He looked as if he were Samoan and easily passed as an NFL defensive tackle. The circumference of his neck bested that of my thigh, or maybe my waist. He caught me staring and nodded toward the monitor that stood before us.

"Watch and listen. This will be your only chance."

"Only chance at..." Before I could finish my question, a face appeared on the monitor; an aged and balding man with round, wire-framed glasses and a bow tie. His smile and eyes were placid, his cheeks rosy. There was a frightening joy about him.

"You are now referred to as Subject 276. Your name has as little meaning as life itself at this point. As you can see around you, there are other test subjects. As you are an astute man, you can probably assume there are two hundred and seventy-five subjects. That would be an understandable assumption. Unfortunately, not all of those test subjects are still alive. What happened to them? Very simple -- they were either eaten or turned."

I attempted to interject, but clearly the video was recorded. The man in the tie marched onward.

"You have a simple task before you. That task? Survive. We've matched you with a cell mate, Subject 144, who is your polar opposite. You were the top surgeon in your field and he was serving three life sentences for multiple murders. You saved hundreds of lives, he took them. But now, you're tasked with saving only one life -- yours. The rules of this study are simple. You will be given only water. At some point, in order to survive, one of you will have to turn to cannibalism. How and when that happens, is up to you. There will be no weapons or implements of any kind. Whoever does survive this test, will move on to another cell mate, until there is only one.

"At that point, the last man standing will be given a new chance at life -- that is, if that particular test subjects wants another chance. As you know, the apocalypse has decimated the population and the moral compass of the human race. It's as brutal on the surface as it is down here. Life is either precious or worthless, depending on your personal philosophy. Oh, and one more thing, in case you need any more incentive to partake of the flesh, should both of you refuse the one directive you have been given, you will be infected with the very virus that has helped to eradicate our race. Good luck, and may the best man feed."

Without so much as a nod, the monitor went black. The man that wheeled the cart out returned.

"Excuse me," I stood as I spoke. "You have to get me out of here. I have a family..."

The man rolling the cart paid no attention to my pleas. He simply rolled the television away and disappeared into the surrounding blackness.

"Now you know. Wish you didn't?" One forty-four broke the silence.

"This is madness," I whispered.

"Damn straight, 276. But it's our madness, our reality. It's you and me in a race to the finish; only the finish line is a dead end buffet. One of us is going to die and the other...well, I don't know if I'd call that surviving or not. But it beats losing; which, by the way, I will not do. You see, I've already been through three other test subjects. That's right; numbers 42, 91, and 104. Just sos ya know, we don't taste like chicken and that first bite will make you sick."

I wanted to speak, wanted to ask questions. My voice, however, had a much simpler plan -- silence.

"Oh, and by the way, you might think it best to just attack and get this nightmare over with right away. They don't like that. They enjoy a good suffering. If I was to tear into you right now, my reward for finishing you off too quick would be getting the juice."

"What is it," my voice exploded from my mouth, "that you mean by *juice*?"

One forty-four Laughed. "I kinda figured you'd be able to put that two and two together, seeing as how you're some kinda fancy ass doctor. Don't worry, I'll hip you to yet another truth."

My cell mate leaned in close and offered a wide, toothy grin. His teeth were yellowed and cracked.

"The juice is what they'll shoot you up with if you ignore their rules. The juice will turn you into one of the damned. It's slow and it's painful as hell. I've watched it turn men bigger than me into pant pissing babies."

One forty-four took in a deep, measured breath. "Trust me, you'd rather die than be juiced."

I wove my fingers into my hair and dug my fingernails into my scalp. "I don't understand. Why are they doing this?"

"Because they can, goddamn it. And you may as well stop asking so many fucking questions. They see and hear everything. You start digging too deeply and they'll cut their losses and send the pain through your veins. Besides, how do you know I'm even telling you the truth? I am going to eat you. I may even do it while you're still alive. That'll sure as shit show those psych-fuck bastards who they're messing with."

"Can you at least…"

One forty-four Shook his head. He was done with words. I took in a breath to speak again and his head tilted and eyes narrowed. At the end of his arms, fists the size of large grapefruits, were clenching into white-knuckle balls.

A gut wrenching scream pierced the surrounding darkness. One forty-four placed his hands together and...

I nearly laughed. "Are you praying? For what? Certainly you cannot believe any sort of God exists at this point. What point does it serve to offer up words of need when clearly the race of man was forsaken long ago? We've suffered profound and irreversible for, what, ten years? Nearly eighty percent of the population is either rotting in wet, sloppy pieces or chasing after the living to crack their skulls on the ground and scoop out their brains. Any God with an ounce of common sense and humanity wouldn't allow that to happen."

One forty-four stood and pulled me from my bed. My feet dangled above the ground.

"If you mock my God one more time, I won't care what they do to me, I'll kill you and praise Jesus as they juice my ass."

"My apologies," was all I could get out through the tourniquet 144 made of my shirt neck.

He dropped me onto my cot. I quickly scrambled to right myself and stare at 144 – every second of every waking moment, if needed.

That's exactly what I did. Stare. Slowly, my mind and body were overtaken by an all-consuming fatigue. Desperately, I wanted to lay down and shut my eyes. Sleep away this nightmare and wake to find it all in the past. But dare I enjoy the luxury of sleep, even for a moment? One forty-four said it himself, they didn't want this to happen too quickly. Surely that could only mean one thing -- at the moment, I was safe.

But for how long? At what point will it be okay to take the life of 144? And...more to the matter...would I be able to do it?

I'll only know if I try.

*

I was drop-kicked out of sleep by a chorus of sadistic screams. The disembodied sounds were quickly followed by maniacal laughter. I sat up and looked across the cell to see 144 waving back and forth, eyes closed, as if he were listening to a majestic symphony composed specifically for him. He didn't even bother to open his eyes before he spoke.

"The sound is beauty. You hear that?" One forty-four opened his eyes and glared at me.

I nodded.

"First the scream. That's the sound of someone realizing what's about to happen to them. Next is the laughter. That's the joyful noise of someone realizing what they are about to do in order to survive. Laughter is life, my friend. Which will spill from between your lips at the end?"

One forty-four Laughed.

I dropped back onto my cot. Every molecule that made up my existence wanted to scream, shout at the top of my lungs, beg for freedom...or forgiveness, whichever would get me out of here first.

Before I could prepare for an honest and meaningful discourse with 144, my stomach turned over and twisted itself into a knot. The pain bubbled up my esophagus and seeped from my mouth.

"Hurts doesn't it? You wouldn't think starvation would hurt. At least I wouldn't. But damn if it doesn't. Feels like something is eating you alive from the inside out. All you want is to stop it, but you can't. You can drink all the water you want, but it never helps. You'd do anything for a steak, a half a chicken, a delicious apple, or...well...just about anything. You don't want your next meal to be the man seated across from you; but you know, at some point, it won't matter.

"When the mind snaps and survival becomes the only directive, nothing else matters."

He continued his diatribe, words forming, falling, and failing to deliver the same message over and over to my ears. It wasn't so much what he said that was beginning to get under my skin, it was how he said it; the flippant way 144 conversed about the inevitable.

I closed my eyes against the strain of looking upon the three hundred and sixty degree panorama of filth and hopelessness. A bright red outline remained behind my eyelids – 144. Numbers. 276. 144.

"How did you do it?" I asked. "Kill numbers 42, 91, and 104? And how much of them did you have to eat until they declared you winner?"

One forty-four Sat up and smiled at me. "Now I can't tell you that, 276. You might steal my best ideas. Some things are best left unsaid. As for how much I had to eat? Let's just say I ate until I was full. Once you've managed to get past the first swallow, the rest is just raw, bloody chicken -- or so your mind insists. After you've 'Hannibal'd' two or three, you start to gain a taste for it."

One forty-four Stood and slowly stalked his way over to me. "In fact, your belly wants it, needs it. You forget about the normal rules of society and all that matters is survival. What is that saying? Oh yeah, 'Do what thou wilt...'"

"Shall be the whole of the law," I finished the familiar quote. "The law of Thelema. I'm familiar with it."

One forty-four Stood back up and carefully made his way back to his bunk. "What, you a devil worshiper or something?"

"You mean, a Thelemite? No. The rest of the law of Thelema states that 'Love is the law.' This isn't referring to hedonism, but acting according to ones own true will, or calling. I don't prescribe to any religion."

"You hate God? What the fuck? Let me guess, you're not even American," 144 spat.

"First, under the circumstances, why would that matter? The boundaries of race and nationality were blown to shit when the virus took hold. Second, what makes you assume I am not American? If you're equating the practice of religion to that of patriotism or nationality, then you really are dumber than I assumed. Although at given times the American people were led by theocracies, our country was not created for theocratic rule."

One forty-four Slowly shook his head. "What in the fuck are you talking about?"

"I was trying to...never mind. As you so eloquently said, it doesn't matter."

My head dropped back on the end of the cot -- the end where a pillow should be. I'd had enough of talk and of listening to the madness of ignorance.

To sleep was that remained. Perchance I would dream...or die in my sleep. At the moment, I'd gladly accept either.

*

Two days ticked by. Three. Five. After a while, I lost count. The only meaningful measure of time now was the twist and knot of my stomach. My body had already begun to display signs of starvation.

Diarrhea and weakness being the most obvious. It seemed every time I tried to stand, I felt a rivulet of warmth slowly flowing down my leg.

I was healthy before I was abducted – marathon level fitness. That would work against me now. Had I a love handle here or a beer gut there, I'd have more stored fat to aid me in survival. As it was, having an OCD about my physical health could be the thing that did me in.

There was no time to revel in irony. I had to form a plan. One forty-four had already done the deed three times. Nothing would stop him from serving me up on a platter. I had to be the one. I had to survive.

When I finally opened my eyes, I glanced over at 144.

Gone.

In his place was a bone-rack of a man with ebony black skin and blood red flame tattoos licking his chest and neck. Protruding from his forehead were the tiniest horns. Between his legs, a tail snaked.

"What are you?"

The creature unleashed a demonic laugh.

"I am your," it paused. "Endgame."

The thing laughed and flames erupted from its mouth. A forked tongue shot out of its mouth and licked ruby red lips that sparkled with flecks of diamond.

"So you are the final stage? What I will become should I..."

"Partake of the flesh," the creature hissed. A thick, sulfuric smoke poured from its nostrils.

I closed my eyes. When they re-opened, 144 was kneeling in front of me, slapping my right cheek.

"Dude, wake the fuck up. You're not dealing well with starvation. I've seen some men break fast, but..."

"Don't say break fast; its too close to breakfast." I nearly laughed at my pathetic attempt at humor. Instead, I put my head in my hands to hide the tears welling in my eyes. I was hallucinating now, which meant I was deep in the throes of starvation. Soon I would grow too weak to do what had to be done.

That meant only one thing.

One forty-four and I sat and stared at one another. I swallowed; every sound of the action amplified by my skeletal frame.

He hummed, 144 did. I didn't recognize the tune and I didn't bother to ask him what it was. It didn't matter. What did matter was my impending frailty and what might wind up being the inability to fight my cell mate off when his over-large, clacking teeth came at me.

Would he at least do me the favor of ending my suffering before he broke open the fava beans? And would he get the reference? Probably not. If I were to break out a chainsaw or hook, that he'd understand.

I shook the cobwebs from my mind. Clarity had to come and had to do so quickly. If there was any hope of me surviving, it would require swift action. One forty-four had to die tonight.

But how? How was a starving surgeon supposed to take down a man who'd served time in prison for murder?

Where there's a necessity, there was always an invention. I had a plethora of knowledge at my disposal. Endless tomes of information filled my brain with the skill set to transplant a lung, do tracheotomies in my sleep.

Mind over matter over mass. Brain had to outwit brawn.

My lower intestine shifted and roared its disapproval. I fought hard not to give into its stabbing pain. The second 144 smelled weakness, he'd strike.

God, listen to me, I thought. Instead of planning an elegant dinner with my wife, I was plotting the death of a cell-mate.

"What do you think they do with the losers?" I asked.

One forty-four Turned to me. I caught a glimmer of pain dance across his face.

"Rumor has it," he started and then paused to suck deep a shocking cramp, "they grind the remains and sell them as a meat product to anyone willing to buy."

"No." I shook my head. "I refuse to accept that conclusion."

"Believe whatever the fuck you want. But what's left out there, the rules of society don't apply. How would you intelligentsia put it...we've devolved into baser creatures."

I laughed, partially to cover the breath-stealing ache that punched me in the gut.

"Well said, my friend."

One forty-four jerked himself into a standing position, his hands clenched into white-knuckle fists. "No. We ain't friends. Never were, never will be. You go down that route and you won't be able to do the deed when the man comes a callin'."

He closed his eyes against the pain. "One way or another, they can't win. This may come as a shock to you, but I've come out alive from three of these...whatever they are...to make sure they didn't win. This isn't about me, or you, or any of the unlucky bastards tucked away down here. This is about showing those sons a bitches they cannot break the human spirit."

I had to admire 144's spirit. It reminded me of the vast majority of Americans who swore they would have their revenge on those who caused 911. The only flaw in that logic is fighting terrorists was like chasing chickens or herding cats; it sounds easy until you actually gave it a go.

"Have you known anyone to get out of here?"

144 Laughed. "Oh yeah. They walked out with cotton candy, coke, and a hooker on each arm. Fuck if I know. I've watched them carry someone to a door and walk them through. That's it. I have no idea what happens behind that door. Are they released back into the wild of the apocalypse, and are they infected first? The only way to know that answer is to survive -- which one of us will do."

Then it hit me, something odd in the mix that 144 hadn't picked up on. Instead of holding this bit of intel, I opted to let it out, hoping it might spin him into a rage and knock him off guard.

"You've survived three times...and yet here you are. Why haven't they sent you through this magical door?"

He smiled at me and nodded slowly.

"Yeah....that's the billion dollar question. Well, lucky for your smart ass, I have the answer." One forty-four held up five fingers to me. "Five killah thrillah. I've got two more to go and I am free as a dream. They'll walk my ass through that door and I'll know for sure if it's freedom or something far worse than death that awaits me. Either way, I'll be out of this miserable existence."

Just then 144 grabbed his stomach, folded over, and dropped to his knees. Another wave hit him and shot his torso up and over his body until he was on his back, hands still grappling with his gut. As he lay there, teeth clenched to near breaking, his exposed throat inspired my next move.

Without a single thought or nod to remorse or guilt, I stood up, lifted my arm, and dropped the full weight of my body, elbow first, onto his neck. I felt the pop and crack of the hyoid bone and surrounding structure.

His esophagus and windpipe were collapsed. It was now only a matter of time before suffocation took 144. I'd done it...survived.

One forty-four looked up at me with bulging eyes. He reached up with one hand, his other busy clawing and scraping at his ruined throat. I made the mistake of looking into his eyes. Desperation made itself home in his pupils. At that moment, I felt something in me snap -- like my soul took a nose dive into depravity. I had fought so long and hard to not give into the apocalypse and its savage mentality. I wanted to go through what remained of my life with grace and dignity. I failed.

One forty-four attempted to speak through his crushed larynx. When he realized the extent of the damage, he mouthed something.

"I don't understand you," I said.

His lips were paling to death's pallor.

He mouthed the words again, slowly this time. I understood.

You have to eat me.

All at once, reality crashed down upon my shoulders. I fell back onto my bunk and wept. It was the last thing I wanted anyone in this dungeon to see of me, but it didn't matter. Nothing else mattered.

"I'm alive," I shouted.

"Alive!" The sound seemed to bounce off the walls with an ironic finality.

I repeated myself, this time an uncontrollable laugh followed the words from my lips.

One forty-four's arm fell to the floor. His chest stopped heaving. He was gone.

I was alone.

"What now? Huh? Do I need to prove myself again? You want more? Bring it. I'm ready now."

The same cart that introduced me to this living hell was rolled out in front of the cell. The guard reached around the cart and depressed a switch. The same, ghost in the machine appeared before me.

He smiled.

I screamed.

"You have nearly claimed victory over your foe. There is but one deed remaining before we move you one step closer to freedom."

"Fuck you," I shouted over the man's voice. Unlike the introductory video, this time he responded.

"I see the cell has broken you of your civility. That is such a predictable shame. The new world order is in short supply of eloquence. I was hoping you might inject a bit of class to these death-row rejects. No matter."

"Go to hell, you twisted, sadistic _"

"Now, now...dare you bite the hand the feeds you?"

He then nodded to the floor of the cell.

"Dinner is served, my friend."

"I'm not your goddamn friend and I will not give into your psychopathic fantasies." My voice was raw. I wasn't sure how many more syllables I could eek out, before my larynx was as useless as the man's on the floor.

"You will be surprised to find out you do have a choice. Either follow the rules and devour a portion of that man, or..." he nodded to the servant that stood sentinel by the cart.

As the man spoke, the servant retrieved a small, black-velveteen box from the cart. Once the box was popped open, the gloved man pulled out a hypodermic and held it aloft.

"What he holds is the very virus that brought the world to its knees. Should you choose to not perform the required cannibalism, you will be injected. The serum will flow through your bloodstream and, within hours, your system will be consumed with the darkest need man has ever known. Before you make your choice, know this...there is no cure. The second that needle pierces the veil of your flesh, all is lost."

The man on the screen released a soft, low laugh that ate at the fabric of my soul. I raced to the bars that separated us and reached my arm toward the cart and the man with the needle.

"I will kill you, I swear." I growled as my hand clawed at the air in vain.

"Tick tock, my good man. It's a simple decision. Eat or evolve."

The simple statement punched me in the empty gut and forced me down to my knees. Tears, snot, and shit raced to the floor. I could feel myself broken, lost without the guidance of grace.

My head fell backwards and a cry of despair issued up into the surrounding darkness. No one would hear me; even if they did, no one would care.

"I'll give you," the man whispered, "thirty seconds to make your choice. When the thirty seconds are up, if your teeth have not torn flesh from bone, you will be infected. Your clock starts now."

Thirty seconds to decide the fate of my sanity. Thirty goddamn seconds to choose between a lifetime of guilt-infested misery or a guiltless, miserable existence. No measure of sanity would allow a man to make that choice.

Who was I kidding? I had no sanity remaining. That was lost the moment I dropped my elbow onto 144's throat.

My decision was made the very second the light in his eyes was extinguished.

I turned my head to take in the cold, dead body before me.

My mouth was bone dry. I tried to lick my lips, but my tongue was like sandpaper against a metal file.

Slowly, I made my way to my hands and knees to pull myself in close to the still-life corpse that was my doing.

"That's it," the man on the screen cheered with a whisper. So much of me wanted to turn and spit into the screen. But the futility of the gesture would only serve to engorge my hatred of what I'd become in this microcosm of mankind. Hatred and chaos reigned supreme and nothing else mattered. It was kill or be killed. I had no other choice at the moment.

Conscience and compassion drained from my life as my fingers wrapped around the dead arm and lifted it closer to my mouth. The stench was unforgiving in its palette. It took every ounce of courage I could conjure to not run and hide as I placed my teeth on the flesh. Immediately I tasted salt and smelled the sour funk of piss and BO.

As I started to bite down, I heard a moan coming from behind. I turned to Mr. Bow Tie glaring at me.

"Stalling? You're down to fifteen seconds."

Instinct took over and I forced my teeth over the meat of the arm and clenched my jaw as hard as possible. The flesh resisted. I had to saw my lower jaw back and forth and jerk my head side to side to finally break through the epidermis.

As soon as my teeth entered the flesh, blood pooled into my mouth. The bitter taste mingled with the acidic tang of bile to create a flavor no man or woman should ever experience.

Another quick jerk of the head and the morsel of flesh pulled away from the bone. I chewed the rubbery bit until it was pulped enough to swallow. As the hunk of human made its way down my esophagus, I went back at the arm like a rabid dog. There was no way I would allow these mad bastards any doubt that I'd completed my task.

But with every bite, I felt less and less human. The taste of raw flesh and blood brought something animalistic to the fore and shut down the governors and filters put in place by years of education, breeding, living, and loving. Slowly, a new directive filled my state of being...

Consume.

I tore into the flesh of the arm as if possessed. Bite after bite I chewed and swallowed, until the whole of the forearm was gone. Without pause, I moved to the bicep...and the shoulder...and the neck...and the chest.

Before I could move down to the meat of the chest, the voice from the monitor called my conscience back.

"Enough. You've proved yourself worthy."

I turned to the man, blood pouring down my chin and chest. "Who is my next opponent?"

The man chuckled. "So, 144 broke the rules and told you more than you were meant to know. No matter...the game is done. However..."

A flood of paranoia and sick washed over me.

"One forty-four clearly neglected to inform you of one crucial matter. He was infected. During his last fight, he failed to feast; so his only option was infection. Now that you've won the bought, it's safe to tell you that the virus is currently coursing through your veins, attaching itself to everything it needs to perpetuate itself.

"As I speak, your very DNA is twisting in upon itself to reform into a wholly foreign structure. I believe you can draw that line of thought to its logical conclusion."

Bow Tie nodded and the man next the cart shut him down and turned to wheel him away. As the cart rumbled across the stone floor, a primal howl boiled up from my gut and assaulted the air around me. My arms convulsed as the raging roar transformed into vomit-inducing sobs.

Against the screen of my eyelids, my life played back in a continuous loop of loss. I had it all; now I have nothing.

As my tears bulleted the stone floor, a choice was born. I had another option -- one that would not only prevent me from becoming another cog in the machine of hate, but would also end the vicious cycle within this nightmare dreamscape.

I stood and shouted.

"There's always another choice."

Snot bubbled at my nostrils and tears raced down my cheeks.

As I stood in the center of my prison, a quote from the late Nelson Mandela came to mind. Through choking sobs, I whispered: "I learned that courage was not the absence of fear, but the triumph over it. The brave man is not he who does not feel afraid, but he who conquers that fear."

In the speaking of the words, I felt fear drain from my being. In that moment, my fear was conquered. My choice was made.

I raised my wrist to my mouth.

I took in one last breath of life.

With the only truth that mattered urging me forward, I did what had to be done.

The taste of my own blood was just as bitter as 144's.

Peace caressed my cheeks as my breathing slowed and my vision tunneled. I had hoped to die with more pomp and grace; my life's work celebrated. But those intangible notions were lost in this bleak world.

My heart struggled. My neck could no longer hold the weight of my head. My bladder released what little liquid remained within my body.

A warm trickle of dignity ran down my leg.

The very last thought to spark from the synapses of my brain was fractured, but profound.

...my own terms.

About Jack

Jack Wallen is a seeker of truth and a writer of words. Although he resides in the unlikely city of Louisville, Kentucky, he likes to think of himself more as an interplanetary soul ... or so he tells the reflection in the mirror. He's also the author of:

I Zombie I

My Zombie My

Die Zombie Die

Lie Zombie Lie

Cry Zombie Cry

Zombie Radio

T-Minus Zero

The Last Casket

Hell's Muse

Screampark

Klockwerk Kabaret

Shero

Shero II: Zombie A GoGo

Shero III: Death by Cosplay

A Blade Away

Gothica

Endgame

If you want to receive an automatic email when Jack's next book is released, sign up on his website jackwallen.com. Your email address will never be shared and you can unsubscribe at any time.

To get more information about Jack Wallen, stop by his website jackwallen.com or send an email to jack@jackwallen.com to chat about his books, music, or cats...or whatever.

Support authors

For any author to succeed, word of mouth is crucial. If you enjoyed Fading Hope, please consider leaving a review at Amazon, even if it's only a line or two; it would make all the difference and would be very much appreciated.